D0475399

Praise for *Switching Gears*

"An emotional tale of finding love after loss. *Switching Gears* boasts a cast of wonderfully flawed characters that grow their way into your heart."
—Kasie West, author of *The Fill-In Boyfriend* and *P.S. I Like You*

"Packed full of competitive spirit and restorative heart."
—Natalie Whipple, author of *House of Ivy & Sorrow* and *Transparent*

Praise for *Love, Lucas*

"Just as readers think they know how this story is going to end, a big plot twist changes the tale's course. . . . Fans of Sarah Dessen and realistic fiction with a poignant and sad slant will find this an enjoyable read."
—*School Library Journal*

"A deeply moving tale of unimaginable loss and the redemptive power of love. Sedgwick masterfully delves into the painful details of losing a loved one, breaking your heart even as her beautiful words stitch you back together. Romance and friendship, true growth and authentic healing, this story blew me away. It takes a special book to bring tears to my eyes *and* make me swoon."
—Rachel Harris, *New York Times* bestselling author of *The Fine Art of Pretending* and *The Natural History of Us*

INTERLUDE

CHANTELE SEDGWICK

Sky Pony Press
New York

This is a work of fiction. Names, characters, places, and incidents are either the products of the author's imagination or used fictitiously.

Sky Pony Press books may be purchased in bulk at special discounts for sales promotion, corporate gifts, fund-raising, or educational purposes. Special editions can also be created to specifications. For details, contact the Special Sales Department, Sky Pony Press, 307 West 36th Street, 11th Floor, New York, NY 10018 or info@skyhorsepublishing.com.

Sky Pony® is a registered trademark of Skyhorse Publishing, Inc.®, a Delaware corporation.

Visit our website at www.skyponypress.com.

10 9 8 7 6 5 4 3 2 1

Library of Congress Cataloging-in-Publication Data is available on file.

Cover design by Sammy Yuen

Print ISBN: 978-1-5107-1515-8
Ebook ISBN: 978-1-5107-1517-2

Printed in the United States of America

To my dad—
For being the greatest example of forgiveness I've ever known.

CHAPTER 1

Life will lead you nowhere,
unless you take its hand and tell it where to go.
—J.S.

I hate waiting. So sitting in this *waiting* room is the worst possible thing I could be doing today.

"Sarah?"

I frown as the girl next to me stands and follows the nurse down the hallway. I know I got here before her; I stood in front of her when I checked in. She probably has the other doctor in this office, but still. It's annoying.

I grab a brochure, glance at the cover, and lean back against the uncomfortable chair

Living with Kidney Disease.

There's a picture of a dad with an arm around his child. They look happy and carefree.

I want to rip it up and stomp on it.

Kidney disease is anything but happy.

"You'd think they were going to Disneyland or something," a voice says.

I glance at the man next to me and stare at him a moment before nodding. "Yes. They're too happy, right?"

1

He smiles. "They need to make those brochures a little more realistic if you ask me." He pushes his hair out of his eyes and sits back in his chair again, still watching me. "'Kidney Disease Sucks' should go on the front."

I think of my sister, Maddy. "Tell me about it."

"How long have you had it?"

I stiffen and glance over at him. "Oh. I . . . uh . . . my sister has it. Not me."

"You're close?"

"Very."

He nods in understanding. "I'm sorry she's suffering. I know how much it sucks."

All I can do is nod and sit there, staring at the brochure, not knowing what to say for once. Sure, it sucks. My sister has it, but I'm healthy. I don't have any right to say anything other than I hate that it's slowly killing her.

And by the way he looks, I'm positive he has the same thing she does. He looks awful. Tired, weak, pale. I want to comfort him somehow, but instead I set the brochure on the empty chair next to me and fold my arms.

Stupid kidneys.

I lean back in my chair, thinking of the old days. Better days. When Maddy could go to school and just be normal. How do things change so fast? And why do they have to change? I hate change.

"Mia?" A nurse stands near the door, a clipboard in her hand and a pencil stuck in her light hair. She glances around the room until her eyes fall on me when I stand.

Finally.

I force a smile and follow the nurse down the hall.

"How are you doing today?" she asks. I've always hated the small talk that goes on in doctors' offices. Just like what's happening now. When the nurse looks like she's having the worst day ever but smiles and fakes happy anyway.

"Good. You?

She shrugs, her back to me. "Just another day."

"I hear ya." Kind of. It's not just another day for me, though. It's the day I save my sister's life. But I don't tell her that. I'm sure she knows why I'm here. It's probably on my chart.

She stops in the hallway near a bathroom door. "Go ahead and step on the scale and I'll get your weight before we go back to your room."

I cringe. "Okay." I always hate this part of the doctor's visit. The weigh-in. It's like I'm on some reality show and everyone can see how many pounds I should lose. I always want to go on a crash diet after. Usually I just stop and get a shake on my way home instead.

I stand on the scale while she writes my weight down on her clipboard and smiles as she makes small talk again.

As I step off the scale, I frown. I probably shouldn't have eaten that Whopper meal for lunch. Or that Chinese food last night.

Oh well. It was worth it—and anything's better than Mom's cooking. Seriously.

"I'll need a urine sample as well." She holds out a cup and I take it. Why doctors are fascinated with pee is beyond me. "You'll be in room 3. Just meet me in there when you're done."

"Sounds great." I step in the bathroom and shut the door.

After I do my business, I head back to the room.

She's there, waiting like she said she would be. She gestures to the examination table and I step up and sit on it. I relax as she takes my blood pressure and asks me a bunch of questions about my health.

"You're eighteen?"

"Yep. Yesterday was my birthday."

"Wow. You're very . . ."

"Determined?" I answer for her.

She nods and types something into the computer before she pushes back in the chair. "The doctor will be in shortly."

As I sit on the examination table, my legs dangling over the edge, I stare at the magazines in a little container by the wall, trying to decide if I want one. By the time I get over there and grab one, though, I'm sure the doctor will walk in. So I just sit, looking forward to the day I get my test results back and I'll be able to tell Maddy that I'm going to save her life.

The door opens and Dr. Mason walks in. "Hello there, Mia. I knew you'd be here after you turned eighteen, but I didn't think it would be the next day." He chuckles and shakes my hand. "You still want to donate your kidney to Madison, right?"

"Yes."

"Your parents approve?"

"Yes. They're worried, of course, but they're support-ing my decision one-hundred percent." Kind of. They want me to think some more before I jump into it. They should know me better than that, though.

He nods. "I'm glad to hear it. Well, we know you both have the same blood type, so that's great. Let me look you over and then we'll take a little more blood from you, run some more tests, and see if you're a match all the way around."

"When will the results be ready?"

"About two weeks."

"Okay." I know I'll be a match. I'm the perfect candi-date. Who would be better than a sister?

No one.

He stares at me a moment, a small smile on his face. "You've read the pamphlet I gave you?"

"Of course."

"So you know what to expect?"

"Recovery is worse on the donor."

"That's right. Donors are also at greater risk for high blood pressure, can be prone to hernias, and may expe-rience pain. I'm not saying these things will happen to you—I just wanted you to be aware of what you're getting yourself into and what *could* happen down the road."

"Will my age affect how my remaining kidney functions?"

He shakes his head. "No. You'll be at a higher risk of reduced kidney function as you get older, but honestly, most donors, especially healthy and young ones, come out just fine and live a happy and normal life. You'll be fine. I just want you to be prepared for the pain after surgery. But what's a little pain when you get to save your sister's life, right?"

I smile. "Right."

CHAPTER 2

Look at me for real and tell me what you see
Pennies for your thoughts if you can see what's haunting me
Loneliness, longing, a life full of lies
Tell me, please tell me, what you see behind my eyes
—J.S.

The parking lot is filled with cars. I curse under my breath when I see some monster SUV in my usual parking space.

"What's the matter?"

I ignore Maddy's question and drum my hands on the steering wheel while I shoot daggers at that white SUV. "Seriously? Don't they know that's my spot? What moron do I have to yell at today?" I frown and glance around for an empty space while Madison chuckles in the passenger seat.

"It's not like your name was on it."

My hands tighten on the steering wheel. Maddy always makes me feel horrible when I say something rude. She's way nicer than me. "Still. They shouldn't make you walk that far."

"It's just across the parking lot, Mia. I'll be fine." She smiles and reaches out to touch my arm. "And I'm sure there are people here sicker than me."

I pull in another spot and put the car in park. "Doubtful."

The dialysis center is one of my least favorite places. Not just because I have to wait for Madison to get her treatment, but because there's so much hopelessness in there. So many people battling the same disease as Maddy. So many people dying a slow and horrible death because they're on that stupid transplant waiting list for too long.

Once I get my results, which should be any day, all that will change. She'll be healthy and we won't have to worry about lists anymore.

"Hey. You gonna come in with me or not?"

I glance over as Maddy opens the door. "Wait." I scramble to get my seatbelt undone. "Let me help you out."

She rolls her eyes. "I'm perfectly capable of stepping out of a car."

I jump out anyway and slam the door before running around to hold on to her arm and help her out.

She frowns as I lead her across the parking lot. "I'm fine, Mia. Seriously. You're freaking me out with all this big-sister stuff."

"That's what I'm here for, so get used to it." I don't let go of her until we go through the building's double doors. I wrinkle my nose at the smell of cleaning products and medicine. Yet another reason I hate it here. A nurse, probably in her thirties, greets us at the check-in desk. "Hello, Madison. You're right on time. Why don't you come on back?"

"Thanks, Jane," Madison says.

I swear she learns the names of every single person she meets. And remembers them. She's been coming here for a few months, but I don't even remember my friends' names half the time, let alone strangers'.

"Let's get your weight real quick," Jane says, stopping halfway down the hall. Maddy hands me her purse and steps on the scale. I keep my eyes on Jane. I don't want to see how much more weight Maddy has lost. Jane frowns a little as she adjusts the scale to get Maddy's correct weight and writes it down. "You can step off." She writes something else on her clipboard and turns down the hall. "Let's go get your blood pressure and temperature."

I wonder why she frowned but decide not to ask. Yet. I'm sure it's just because of her weight, but what if it's something worse? Like Maddy could use more bad news.

Jane leads us back to the dialysis room. There are beds and recliners everywhere with red tubes stuck in every occupant's arm. I can't stand the whirr of the machines or how bright the lights are. And the sound of voices humming through the room reminds me how crowded it is in here. It makes me feel like Maddy is on display for everyone to see. Which she is. You'd think they'd have a little more privacy, but no.

"Hi, Ruthann," Maddy says as she passes an older lady reading a magazine. "How have you been?"

Ruthann looks so fragile with her wrinkled skin and big purple veins poking out of her hands. She sets the magazine down, her eyes finding Maddy. "Madison, it's good to see you. I'm good. First time in this week? I didn't see you on Monday."

"I had an appointment with my doctor."

Ruthann frowns. "Everything good I hope?"

Maddy just shrugs and Ruthann reaches out and pats her on the hand. "You hang in there, darling girl."

"Thanks, Ruthann. You too. I'll see you later."

We finally reach Maddy's station and she sits in the recliner and leans back, ready for her treatment.

"Did you bring anything to do today?" Jane asks.

Maddy pulls a book out of her purse.

"Oooh, I love that one."

Maddy runs her fingers over the cover. "I haven't started it yet, but I've heard it's good." She gives Jane a tiny smile, but I can tell she's just being nice. I know her real smile and that's not it.

Jane keeps making small talk as she gets her equipment ready, and Maddy holds out her right arm, chiming in only when she's asked a question. She's used to this. She comes in three times a week, after all, but I still turn away as Jane hooks her up to the machine.

I'm not scared of blood. I don't pass out when I see it or anything like that. But seeing IVs and tubes sticking out of Madison has always made me nauseous. Maybe because she's my sister and I know how sick she is? Maybe because I can't stand to see her in pain? I don't know. Whatever the reason, I focus on something else until they get the gauze and tape wrapped around her arm.

"You okay?" Maddy asks as I sit in the chair next to her.

I stare at her. She's the one in pain and she asks if *I'm* okay. "I'm good." I grab two magazines out of the stand next to us and put them on my lap, trying to avoid looking at the red tube in her arm.

She picks up her book, but instead of reading it, she sets it on the table next to her after Jane walks away.

I sit up straight and touch her hand. "Are *you* okay?"

Her eyes open and she shrugs. "I'm fine. Just tired." She closes her eyes again and I sit back in my chair. She's never this . . . down. Normally she's all peppy and happy. Joking around with the nurses. Something's up.

"You don't want to talk about it?" I try, hoping she doesn't shut off and stop talking to me.

"I told you, Mia. I'm fine. I'd just rather sleep during my treatment today."

"Okay . . ."

"You should take a nap, too. We have three hours. And you look more tired than I feel. And that's saying something."

I touch my face and frown. I don't look that bad, do I? Because when people say you're tired, usually you look horrifying. "Thanks?"

She settles into her chair and doesn't say anything for a while. Which makes for a deeper frown on my face. I've shared a room with her long enough to know the exact second she falls asleep, and the whole time we sit here, I know she's awake. Listening to the conversations around us. Or thinking about . . . something.

It makes me nervous.

Instead of worrying about her, I glance around the open room to distract myself but end up staring at the green curtains that line the windows. Booger green curtains. Seriously. This facility is pretty new, so you'd think they'd get a better decorator.

I notice a man across from us reading a magazine, not bothered at all by the tubes hooked to his arm. Or the fact that everyone else can see him. He glances up, meets my eyes, and watches me. I give him an awkward smile before I look away and shift in my chair, my cheeks heating. I don't like being stared at or being the person doing the staring.

Most of the patients don't seem uncomfortable at all with all the people around. They're used to it. They just sit in their chairs or lay in their beds and read or stare into space.

I notice a little girl, maybe eight or so, in a chair a few rows down. She's watching cartoons while her mother reads. I can't help but feel sorry for her. For both of them.

I honestly wish I could help every one of them. So many people could be saved from something as simple as a kidney transplant. I wonder why more people don't do it.

I guess it's a little terrifying to give away an organ, though. But if it can save my sister, I wouldn't have it any other way.

Three hours later, we're on our way home. Madison is quiet in the passenger seat, and I keep my eyes on the road, my hands clenched tight on the steering wheel while I worry about her.

After forever, she speaks. "Thanks for taking me today. I know that you have better things to do."

"No I don't." Really. I don't.

Her hands are folded in her lap, but then she reaches over and grabs my hand. "Three hours just sitting there has got to get so boring for you. I know how you hate being stuck in places."

"It's fine. I get the spend the day with you, so that's a bonus perk."

"I wasn't much company today. Sorry about that." She folds her arms, the bright purple band covering her dialysis site standing out against her skin. "But really. Thank you for everything you do for me. I'm so lucky to have you as a sister."

I glance over at her pale face, wondering where this sudden emotion and . . . Thankfulness is coming from. "Are you sure you're okay? You're being weird today, Maddy. It's kind of freaking me out."

She sighs. "The doctor says I'm in the final stage of kidney disease. Renal-failure. Did you know that?"

"Yes." Of course I knew that. I was there when he told us. The worst day of my life so far.

"That means I don't have very much longer."

I swallow, pushing the emotion away. I can't let her see me cry. I have to be brave for her. "I'm going to be a match, Maddy. I'll save you. You know this. We've talked about this a thousand times. You're going to be fine. Okay? Please stop talking like you're dying."

She nods. "I'm sorry. And I know I'm going to be okay. I just . . . Wanted to tell you how much I appreciate you. Just in case, you know?" She sits back in her seat and doesn't say anything the rest of the way home.

I keep my eyes on the road, my fingers aching from clutching the steering wheel so tight, but I can't help it. This talk . . . it isn't like her. I can't handle it.

Maddy's the one who's supposed to be strong. Maddy's the one who has always had an unshakable confidence that she'll be all right and things will work out. My own confidence where Maddy is concerned is shaky at best. I don't know why she was the one chosen to go through this. There may be a purpose to all of it, but seeing her go through so much . . . It's done nothing to strengthen my hope that all will be well. Hopelessness has chased it away.

And that troubles me.

Because with hope and a little faith, all things are supposed to be possible. Things end up being okay in the end. But in this case, I fear it isn't enough. Nothing I do or believe is enough.

And all I want to do is cry.

CHAPTER 3

Silence is empty, happiness is fleeting.
Don't know who to turn to, just hope my heart keeps beating.
—J.S.

The house smells like something's burning when we walk through the door, and I know immediately Mom's been cooking. Which in itself is weird, but weirder since it's only four. Dad's setting the table when we make it to the kitchen and I glance around. "What's going on?"

Dad smiles. "Mom's in one of her . . . uh . . . moods."

"Oh, stop it Russ," she says, nudging him with her shoulder.

One of Mom's moods? Oh no. "Maddy, we should have gone to get a hamburger or something before we came home."

She stares at Mom, who's now stirring something in a pot on the stove. "Agreed."

Mom turns around, untying the apron around her waist and letting her auburn hair down. "You guys, it's fine. You're going to love it. It's just a new soup recipe. Healthy."

I groan at the word *healthy*. Ever since Mom started going to the gym, she's been making us new recipes. And ninety percent of them are just nasty. And by the looks of that soup, I'm pretty sure we're going to have to choke it down. I glance around the room. "Hey. Where's—"

"Mia! Maddy!"

Our six-year-old brother Zack zips into the kitchen and almost tackles me to the floor. "Did you bring me a treat?" He bounces on his feet as he holds some kind of Lego creation in his hand.

"No." I shake my head and give him a sad face. "Sorry, bud."

"Oh." His shoulders sag and he mopes to his chair to sit down at the table.

I give him a minute to be sad and then pull a sucker out of my pocket. "Oh, c'mon! Of course I did."

His freckled face lights up and I chuckle as he gives me another hug.

"After dinner," Dad says as he helps Mom put food on the table.

I can't help but watch Zack. He's so full of energy and life. Not to mention, he looks exactly like Mom. Red hair and all. Like her mini-me except he's a boy.

Me and Maddy? We don't look like either of our parents. Well, I guess we have Dad's lankiness, and I'm pretty sure I have his thin lips and small mouth, but our Mexican features—dark hair, brown eyes, and tanned complexions—come from our birth mom. I mean, I'm all about not having pasty white skin, and our heritage may be pretty cool if I knew anything about it, but I hate that it reminds me of the woman I don't remember.

I shake my head and put her out of my mind. We don't talk about her.

Ever.

Maddy sits down at the table and lays her head on her folded arms.

"You okay, Madison? How was your dialysis today?" Dad asks. He pats her back and she sits back up. "It was fine. I'm just tired."

"You're usually tired when you get home, but you look a little paler than normal tonight. Do you want to go lie down? I'll make you anything you want." He glances at Mom, but she doesn't seem to be paying attention.

"I'm fine. Thanks, Dad."

I shoot her a glare across the room and she glares back. She's anything but fine.

He turns to me then. "Mia, I haven't heard you play the piano for a few days. What's going on?"

"I've been busy. Sorry."

He frowns. "If you don't practice, you'll—"

"Lose your gift," I finish as I roll my eyes. "I know, Dad. I'll practice later." My phone rings then, and I go in the other room to answer. My caller ID says UNKNOWN, but I push TALK anyway. "Hello?"

"Mia Cox?"

"This is she."

"This is Dr. Mason's office."

My heart speeds up. The results. They have the results. I smile. "Oh. Hi. Is everything okay?"

"Yes. We just wanted to call and tell you, we have your results from the other day." She pauses for a second and my stomach drops. She paused. If it was good news, she wouldn't have paused. "I'm sorry to say, but you aren't a match for your sister."

I almost drop the phone and it takes me a second to recover. "What?" I whisper.

"You're not a match. I'm sorry, sweetie."

Sweetie. She called me *sweetie.* Why would she do that? Especially since she just gave me the worst news of my entire life. I let it go, though. I can't think straight enough to come up with something snarky. All I can manage is, "Oh. Okay. Thanks."

"If you'd like to come talk to Dr. Mason, he'll be in tomorrow afternoon. Come anytime between 8:00 and 4:00. He'll be happy to explain your results to you."

My brain and voice won't cooperate and all I can do is nod. I hang up without saying good-bye and stare at the phone for a long time.

"Mia?" Mom says from behind me. "You coming to eat? Dinner's ready. I wanted to talk to you about—"

I turn around and shock registers on her face, probably from what she sees on mine. "What is it, honey? What's wrong?" She takes a step forward and I don't move. I just replay the conversation with Dr. Mason's nurse over and over again in my head. "Mia, talk to me."

I stare at the phone again as Mom calls Dad in the room. "Honey?" he says, taking the phone from my hand. "Mia, what happened? Who was on the phone? Are you okay? Is one of your friends hurt or something?"

I shake my head and try to focus, but I'm lost in my own thoughts. I feel pieces of myself falling away. Like I'm made up of tiny beads from a necklace that has been broken and scattered across the floor, knowing even if the pieces are found and restrung, I'll never be quite right again.

This wasn't supposed to happen. I was Maddy's only hope. I was going to make her whole again and she could go back to being the bright sixteen-year-old she was before. Now what? What am I supposed to do to save her now?

"Mia. Look at me, honey." Dad's soft voice fills my senses, pulling me back to myself. When I try to focus on him, though, my eyes fall on Maddy, who's standing in the kitchen doorway. Her eyes are filled with worry, and then, as she gets a good look at my face, something changes. Her expression softens and she nods at me.

She knows.

"It's okay, Mia," she says. She moves around my worried parents and wraps me in a hug. "It's okay. You tried. I'm okay. We'll be okay."

I don't lift my hands to hug her back. I'm in too much shock to move. It's not okay. The reason Maddy was going to live was because of me. And now she has no chance. None. No one in our family is a match. And the only person who was supposed to be was me. I can't save her now.

The realization hits me full force and it almost knocks the wind out of me.

I can't save her.

Dad moves Maddy away, concern etched on his face when she doesn't tell him what's going on. "What is it, honey? Please. Talk to me."

I stare at his tattooed arms. The arms that held me and Maddy when we were babies. The ones that wrapped me in hugs and chased away the monsters in my room when I was a child, when I didn't have a mother to do the same. I stare at them, a lump in my throat, and blink back tears. "I'm not a match." It's barely a whisper, but he hears me, because the next thing I know, he's holding me.

I'm not a match.

CHAPTER 4

A shadow, a whisper, a face in my dreams.
These monsters surround me, mocking, laughing.
They swirl inside until my soul breaks.
And then I fall.
—J.S.

I'm being ridiculous. I know it. But I hole up in my room while my family tries to make Maddy feel better.

It's her life that's going to be over, after all.

Unless a miracle happens and she moves up the transplant list. Which we all know most likely won't happen.

She's going to die. Because of me. Why her? What has Maddy ever done to deserve this? I know we have trials in this life, but you'd think after all the praying we've been doing, we'd get a little slack or something.

I stare out the window as the rain sprinkles down, leaving silent shadows on the sidewalk below. It's so . . . Temporary. Rain. It comes down in sheets, soaking everything in its path, and then it dries up, not leaving any trace of itself anywhere.

Kind of like a human life. We're everywhere, and then

in a split second, we're not there anymore. We disappear and it's like we weren't there at all.

Maddy will disappear. And leave me behind.

I know in my heart she won't be gone for good. A part of her will always be with me, watching over me from Heaven, but it's not the same. I can't let it go. I can't just let her die.

I lean forward and press my forehead to the window. The dark clouds swirl in the sky as the rain falls harder. It's like the weather knows exactly how I'm feeling.

My mood isn't getting any better while I sit and stare out the window, so I sit back down on my bed and let out a slow breath to calm the tension rolling through my body. Sitting in the fetal position for hours on end did a number on my muscles.

While I stretch out my legs again, I shift my attention back to the pile of stuff in front of me and dig through my box of childhood memories, determined to find what I'm looking for. I haven't looked inside for years. I started putting stuff in when I was five—when I realized my life was a little different than most of my friends.

I stare at the old shoebox. My name's glued on the front with silver glitter that chafes off every time I open it. I still can't believe it has held together after all these years. It's funny how oftentimes the most important parts of ourselves end up in something as simple as an old and worn-out cardboard box.

I pull out an old journal and cringe as I read the first page. I was so weird in middle school. Awkward and ridiculously boy crazy. I set the journal to the side to read later and dig deeper, knowing what I'm searching for lies somewhere near the bottom of the box.

If Dad knew what I was doing, he'd probably ground me for the rest of my life.

But I have to do this. It's the only way to save my sister.

More elementary school pictures, report cards, and random papers end up on my bed, including old book reports and old stories I wrote. Why on earth Dad kept my book reports is beyond me. I will say, though, that some of my drawings are totally legit. I should study art in college.

After sorting through a pile of old papers, I finally find it. My name is still scrawled on the front. I recognize the handwriting the moment I see it. Messy. Like mine. Lots of curves and swirly lines. I pull the faded envelope from the bottom of the shoebox and hesitate just a second before opening it.

The birthday card is still in good shape, which surprises me, seeing how it's fifteen years old. The ink is a little faded, but I can read the message clearly.

To. Mi pequeno amor.
Happy Birthday Mia.
Love, Mom

Mi amor. Right. I roll my eyes and fight the urge to black that little sentence out with a Sharpie. I may not speak Spanish fluently, but I do know what that means. And I'm anything but her *love*. I pick up the envelope again and set the card down. The return address is still on the front, along with her name. Carmen Santalina. New York City, New York.

I wonder if she's still in the same apartment, but I'm doubting it.

I slide off the bed and take a deep breath. There's only one way to find out.

Time to face Dad.

♫

He's in the garage working on his '67 Chevy, per usual. He's been working on that car for at least ten years. I think he takes his time fixing it because it's his baby and he doesn't want it to grow up and drive away or something.

The garage door is open, and the smell of paint and motor oil hits my nose. I'm sure other people would cringe at the smell, but I'm used to it. It reminds me of home. Of him.

"Hey, Dad."

He glances up, his eyes widening when he sees me, and smiles. "Glad to see you're out of your bedroom today."

"Yeah, I know. Sorry." Not really.

"You okay now?" He ducks back down under the hood and I hear something twisting.

"I'm fine." I take a step forward, my question hovering on the tip of my tongue. "What ya working on today?"

"Engine."

"Oh. I thought you fixed that a while ago."

I hear him chuckle. "Nope."

"Okay." I stand there, listening to the sound of his tools and his low voice humming along to some classic rock song on the radio. "Uh . . . Dad? Can I talk to you for a sec?"

He pokes his head up again. "Yeah. What's up?"

"I have a question for you."

He raises an eyebrow. "Okay? Sounds serious." He winks, but I'm pretty sure he won't be winking when I ask the question.

"Does Carmen still live in New York?"

The second I say her name, his whole body tenses and he frowns. "I haven't heard from Carmen in years, honey. I have no idea."

"There's no way to find out?"

"I don't know. Her family's there, but . . ." He disappears under the hood again once more, then he straightens, sets his tool down, and hits the MUTE button on the radio before he walks over to me. He wipes his hands on a greasy, disgusting towel and looks me over before folding his arms. "What's this about, honey?"

"I don't know."

"You do. I know that look in your eye. It's the one that puts my whole parenting sense on alert."

"Dad."

"I've seen it many times, Mia. Just tell me. What's going on?"

I try to tell him, but it comes out quiet and in a jumbled mess. "I was just . . . I wanted to . . . Maddy . . ." I don't know how to ask. The words won't come.

He shakes his head and a sigh escapes his lips. He

wipes his forehead with the back of his hand and studies me with . . . pity, I decide. "She won't do anything, Mia."

I twist my hands together. "How do you know?"

"I just do."

"But how?"

Another sigh. This one deeper and more agitated than before. I know I'm pushing him, talking about Carmen. I should stop, but I can't. "She hasn't been a part of your lives for fifteen years. She won't start caring now."

I frown. "What if we told her, though? Does she even know how sick Maddy is?"

"Mia," he runs a hand through his dark hair, his frown deepening.

"I could just call her. Tell her what's going on. Maybe if she knows what's happening to Maddy, she'll—"

"She doesn't care!"

Dad doesn't yell. Ever. So when his voice echoes through the garage, my eyes grow wide and I back away. He's breathing hard, but when he sees how his outburst affects me, his expression softens. "Honey, I'm sorry. It's just . . ." He closes his eyes, pinches the bridge of his nose with his fingers, and takes a deep breath before looking at me again. "She left us. Plain and simple. And that's all I'm going to say about it." He starts toward his car again, and turns the radio back on as I stand there, my eyes burning. "Do you need anything else?" He doesn't look at me, just stands there with his hands on his hips, staring at his stupid engine.

I want to beg him for a recent address or something so I can write to her at least, but I've worn out his patience for the day. So instead I frown, my hands clenching into fists by my side as anger courses through my body. "No," I snap, my temper flaring. "You can go back to working on your stupid car. Sorry to bother you over something so trivial. I thought you'd want to do everything in your power to save your daughter's life, but I guess I was wrong."

His mouth falls open and I swear his eyes tear up.

I should apologize. I know he'd do anything for Maddy, but I don't say another word. Before he can say anything, and before I say anything *else* that I'll regret, I run back inside, ignoring his voice as he calls my name behind me.

When I slam the garage door, I hear Maddy call my name from the living room. I storm around the corner and see her lounged on the couch, reading a magazine. She raises an eyebrow. "Temper?"

"Yes."

She nods. "Go eat something. That usually means you're hungry."

"Does not." She stares at me and I sigh, defeated. "You're probably right."

"There's cheesecake in the fridge."

"Awesome." I go grab a slice and take it straight to my room. Dad comes inside just as I reach the bottom of the stairs and calls for me again, but I ignore him.

Once I slam my door, hoping he hears it, I open my laptop and google "Carmen Santalina in New York City."

Two names come up. Which is better than ninety-six, so that's good. I don't like going behind Dad's back, but if worse comes to worst, I'll have to come up with a plan. Something stupid probably, but at least I care enough about Maddy to try. I can try to get a hold of Carmen. Try both phone numbers. That shouldn't be a big deal, right? One of them has to be her.

What a phone call to receive, though. Or make. A long-lost daughter calling her runaway mother to ask for a body part. Sounds . . . morbid. And I'll admit . . . A little awkward. Desperate? I'll have to talk myself up before I do it. Because I can do it. I talk to people on the phone all the time.

Does texting count, though? I don't think so.

I freeze as I hear someone coming down the stairs and close my laptop before Dad figures out what I'm doing. But Dad doesn't open my door. Maddy does.

"Hey," I start, then freeze.

Her skin is pale, and I know by the look on her face that something's wrong.

My heart speeds up as she wraps her hand around the door frame and looks at me with wide eyes. My whole body goes on alert. "Maddy? Are you okay?"

"I don't know." She shakes her head, still staring at me.

I uncross my legs and put my laptop down. "What do you need?"

"I think . . . I'm gonna . . ."

I'm jumping off the bed before she finishes her thoughts. Her eyes roll back in her head as she collapses and I catch her before her head hits the floor. I fall backward, with most of her weight on top of me, and smack my head on the doorframe.

"Dad!" My head is fuzzy as I scream and try to maneuver out from beneath her. I check to see if she's breathing first, pushing down the panic that's taking over my senses. She is, but it's shallow. And she's pale. So pale.

I hear the garage door open and slam shut. "Mia?" Dad's shout echoes through the house. "Mia? What's wrong?"

"Dad, down here!"

Running footsteps echo through the kitchen and then he's coming down the stairs. He turns the corner and hurries toward us, still sprawled on the floor at the end of the hall. "What happened?"

"Maddy passed out. I don't know . . . She's so pale. What do I, Dad? I don't know what to do!" I set her head on the floor and try to keep myself from hyperventilating. Her dark hair is splayed around her face and she looks like death.

Dad's bent down next to me in two seconds, listening to Maddy's heartbeat, checking her breathing, all the while with his phone in his hand. I don't know who he's talking to, I don't know what he even says, I just keep my fingers on Maddy's pulse, feeling the slowness of her heartbeat and praying it doesn't stop.

Dad's so calm as he talks to the person on the other end. All businesslike, without a trace of panic in his voice. Like nothing's wrong and everything's going to be okay. When he's finished talking, he hangs up and turns to me. "Mia. I need you to call Mom at work. Tell her to meet me and Maddy at the hospital."

I barely remember standing. I don't remember calling, but there's a phone in my hand and Mom's crying on the other end. The conversation is short and I hang up, standing as Dad pulls me out of the way.

Sirens wail in the distance, getting louder and louder until they stop when they reach the driveway. Red and blue ambulance lights flicker outside my window as Dad races to the front door.

Paramedic's swarm the stairs and down the hall to where Maddy still lies, and I find myself backed into the corner, kneeling with my arms folded as I rock back and forth. I don't cry. Not yet. There'll be plenty of time for that later. All I can do is watch as the paramedics hook her up to several wires and tubes and carry her down the hallway and up the stairs on a stretcher.

I get to my feet, my body shaking as Dad puts both hands on my shoulders. I think he knows I'm in shock. "Mia, are you with me?" A nod is all I manage. "Good. I'm going with them to the hospital. Stay here and call your brother. He's at Jacob's house. See if he can stay there tonight. We'll call you when we know what's going on." He wraps me in a quick hug and runs down the hall after the paramedics.

I stare at the doorway, listening to his footsteps fade away. The panic hits me then, and I bury my face in my hands as the front door slams.

Then everything's quiet.

And I'm alone.

CHAPTER 5

Under the glamour and the fame
It was all a ruse, it was all a game
Who was I to believe you were tame?
You put on quite a show
I thought my feelings would be spared
You said you loved me, said you cared
How could you throw away all we shared?
You put on quite a show
All I see is you in his arms
Glitz and money, his good looks and charms
How did your actions not raise my alarms?
You put on quite a show
—J.S.

Maddy looks so peaceful when she sleeps. And not in a creepy way. She's just like that all the time. At peace with the world and everyone around her. She's especially at peace with herself. She never thinks, says, or listens to the negative. Only positive. Always so positive. Even though she's dying at just sixteen, she still finds a reason to smile.

I wish I could be like that.

Her eyes flutter open and she's disoriented for a second before she turns to look at me, lifting the arm with the IV tube sticking out of it to grab my hand with her own. "Mia." She smiles. "I knew you'd be here. You always are."

"Of course. How are you feeling?"

"Eh." She moves around, getting comfortable. "Thanks for stopping my fall. I passed out, didn't I? I knew I was going to. Sorry if I . . . uh . . . startled you."

She's apologizing? Is she crazy? "Don't apologize." I pause. "But I'm not gonna lie. You seriously freaked me out today. Probably the most you've freaked me out . . . ever, actually."

She takes a shaky breath and pushes the button next to her to lift the top half of her bed so she's sitting up. "I know. I didn't mean to."

"Sure you did." I roll my eyes.

She laughs. "You're right. It *was* my body, so I secretly planned for it to pass out in front of you like that." We both laugh, but after a second she shuts her eyes and shakes her head. "Sorry. Still a little dizzy."

I squeeze her hand. "Do you feel okay other than that?"

She shrugs. "I've been better, I think."

"I know."

She lets out a slow breath as she glances at the monitors hooked up to what seems like every part of her. "You know, it will be nice when all this is over."

"What do you mean?" She better not mean what I think she means.

She smiles. Not a happy smile, but more of that "at peace" stuff she gives off. "We both know I'm not going to make it."

"Maddy . . ."

"No, really. I just want you to know . . ." She clears her throat and blinks as her eyes well up with tears. "You're the best sister I could have ever asked for. All of our memories. We've had a lot of fun, haven't we?"

I'm shaking my head, tears slipping down my cheeks as I stare at the blankets on her bed. I can't look at her when she's saying this. I don't want to remember her like this. I want her to be healthy again. Perfect like she was when we were growing up. "Please, don't. You can't say good-bye right now. You're not going to die."

"It's okay, Mia. I'm not afraid. I've never been afraid. I've always wondered what Heaven will be like. I imagine it's beautiful and wonderful. I know I'll be okay there, you know?"

"Maddy, please." I want her to stop. I can't handle this right now.

She keeps talking, oblivious to my protests. "I'm not going to find a donor soon enough. We both know it. The doctors know it. Believe it or not, a lot of people are just as sick or sicker than me with this same stupid disease and need a kidney more than I do."

"No." I'm shaking my head. "You need one just as much as they do, if not more." No one deserves a kidney more than she does. She holds this family together. She's the only person I've been able to count on in my whole life. Besides Dad and Mom. But they can't help her. And neither can I. I think of that box on my bed and that faded envelope from earlier. There could be a solution.

Maddy squeezes my hand again. "I don't. I'd rather someone else get a chance to live. It's too late for me."

My head snaps up. "It's not too late." A crazy idea is forming in my head. One that is a last resort, but one I'm determined to make happen. I just need to figure out how. And gather enough courage to go through with it.

"What? What are you thinking right now?" Maddy asks, a curious look on her face.

I lean closer to her. "It's never too late, Maddy, and I'll prove it. I swear to you, you'll be okay. You're going to live and things will be just like they were before you got sick."

"What are you planning to do? You always get that look when you're plotting something and it's never a good thing."

"Don't worry about me. It's not a bad thing at all. It's a good thing. Something that will help you. *Someone* who can help you."

"Mia . . ." She frowns.

"I have to do this. For you. I promised I'd save you, and I'm going to. Just . . . Trust me, okay?"

"Okay." She bites her lip, a nervous look on her face. "Just . . . promise you won't do something stupid."

"Nothing stupid. Promise." My voice cracks on the last word and tears trail down Maddy's cheeks as I look at her. I take in her features, praying she'll hang on until I get back.

"Pinky promise?" She smiles as I hook my pinky with hers.

"Pinky promise."

♬

The house is quiet when I get home, and instead of wallowing in self pity and crying some more, I head straight to my bedroom. My laptop still sits where I left it and I open it, writing down the two addresses I found earlier. I can handle two.

I go to the closet and grab an old backpack stuffed on the top shelf. Not quite a suitcase, but it will work. I put a few changes of clothes inside, pajamas, my phone charger, and some other things I might need. Hopefully the hotel has shampoo and stuff. It should, right?

I scribble a note to my parents, letting them know where I'm going, and set it on the kitchen table. They won't find it for a while. They'll be at the hospital, and Zack is staying with his friend tonight, so it gives me a few hours' head start before they freak out and try to stop me. It feels wrong to do something so drastic, but it's all I can think of. And I'm desperate.

The hallways seems to lengthen as I leave my room. Like I'm doing a walk of shame or something. I glance at our family pictures, especially the ones with Maddy smiling, happy and healthy. It's going to be like that again. I know it. After lingering in front of our most recent one, I hitch my bag on my shoulder and turn the corner.

My grand piano sits untouched in the music room and my fingers twitch, wanting to play. I walk over to it, run my fingers over the keys, and play a short piece I memorized last year for good luck. The music calms me some, and once the song ends, I let my fingers linger on the notes as they fade into the silence of the house.

A new energy fills my soul. I stand up straight, take a deep breath, and walk out the door.

The next time I see my family, I'll have my birth mom with me. And Maddy will be okay. She'll live.

My car waits for me in the driveway and I'm thankful no one's home. I can't believe how easy this is. Now, if I can just calm my nerves, everything will be perfect.

That's the only thought that occupies my mind as I get in my car, peel out of the driveway, and head toward the airport.

CHAPTER 6

I see through your troubled tears
Let me take away your fears
Tell me how to make things right
Chase darkness away, leaving only light
—J.S.

I love being spontaneous, but sometimes, imagining what consequences will await me when I actually do said spontaneous thing makes me question my motives. Though saving my sister is motive enough, but defying Dad to do it? I'm going to be grounded forever.

I stare at the plane ticket in my hand. My parents won't freak out until later when they find my little note, but waiting for them to find it is kind of stressing me out. Maybe I should call them instead.

Then again, I really don't want to suffer their wrath right now. So, I wait for the ticket lady to call my seat number and watch the crowds of people carrying luggage, trying to find their gates. One lady walks by wearing dark sunglasses, a tiny red dress, and four inch heels, dragging a rolling suitcase behind her. Pretty sure every man in the vicinity turns to watch her. I wonder who she is, where she's going. I've always gotten a kick out of people-watching. Not staring, just watching. Inconspicuously.

An older couple walks by, hands held tight together. The man takes great care to help his wife shuffle down the terminal, not getting frustrated at her slow pace. A cute little family comes next, three kids holding hands and trailing after their mother. Then I spot a dad pushing a little girl on top of a large, rolling suitcase. When she tumbles off, he gives her the sweetest hug ever, and I reach in my purse and pull out a pen and a notebook. Instead of staring at everyone and creeping people out, I'll make a list to pass the time. Lists calm me down more than anyone will ever know.

Super weird. I know.

My pen hovers over the paper while I figure out what kind of list to write. I chew on the end of it a second before I start to write.

Reasons my parents are going to kill me.

Yes. That will work nicely.

Reason 1: I'm going on an airplane and flying clear across the country without Mom and Dad's permission. But I'm 18 now. It's cool. I can do stuff like this. I guess I've only been 18 for a few days though, so . . . Yeah . . .

Reason 2: The money I spent on one of the last available seats on this flight was from Gram. To use for college. (Don't tell her. Ever.)

Reason 3: I'm going to see my birth mom. Still not sure what I'm going to say to her. And I really really hope she speaks

English. Which is a dumb thing to worry about, seeing how she married my English-speaking dad.

Reason 4: I have no idea where I'm going to stay or where the heck Carmen even lives, but I'll figure it out. Hopefully.

Reason 5: I'm irrational. That's what Dad will say. And yes. I am.

Just as I start a list of punishments they might inflict, a woman's voice on the loud speaker echoes through the terminal.

"First boarding call for Flight 234 to New York. Rows 1 through 10 may board now."

My heart pounds even though they haven't called my row yet. The rational part of my brain tells me to go home. But I'm not rational. Not today.

People around me stand as they check their tickets and, thankfully, it's not my turn yet. I can freak out some more before I have to make myself walk over there.

Why am I freaking out so much? It's not like I'm doing something horrible. Trying to save someone's life isn't a bad thing. But I have to admit, this is pretty huge. I've never done anything like this in my whole life.

There was that time when I was fifteen when I took Dad's car for a joyride with Maddy in the back seat, but we only went around the block a few times, so it wasn't that big of a deal. Although Dad did ground both of us for a month. I still think he overreacted.

I sit there a moment, thinking of Maddy. If she knew what I was doing, she'd beg me to stay. Beg me not to waste my time tracking down our lost-cause mother. But

I can't think about that now. I'll do anything for her. And I have to do this.

A line forms at the door to the jetway, and people file onto the plane. I watch the line shorten and shorten and my heart speeds up again as the woman taking tickets gets on the intercom. "Boarding call for rows 1 through 20 on Flight 234 to New York. You may board now."

I grab my purse and my backpack holding all of my belongings and head over to the gate. My hand shakes as I give the lady my ticket.

"Have a nice flight," she says with a smile.

"Thanks." I follow a few passengers down the jetway and try not to freak out when I enter the plane. A million thoughts zip through my head and I take slow breaths to try to remain calm.

The plane is bigger than I expected, but I guess I don't have anything to compare it to. Rows of tan seats are all down the aisles, and a super happy stewardess points me to the middle where I'm guessing my seat is.

It's stuffy in here. I hope they have air conditioning since it's like a billion degrees outside.

I scoot past a few people putting their belongings into overhead compartments and finally find my seat. It's by the window, so I stuff my carry-on in the overhead compartment before I sit down with my purse on my lap. I unzip it and pull out the card from Carmen and my cell. My eyes skim the envelope again for the fifth time this morning. I fold it back up and stare at my phone, waiting for the frantic calls of my parents.

Nothing yet, so I turn it off, my stomach churning at what I'll find when I turn it back on again when I land.

Satisfied, I sit back in the seat and wait for take-off. Flying to New York from California is going to take forever, but I'm going to be fine. I'll relax on the plane until we land, then I'll scour New York City all day and all night if I have to. If it turns into weeks, I'll still search. And I won't leave until I find her.

Foolproof plan if you ask me.

Then again, I haven't always been the best at planning.

You'll be fine. Calm the heck down.

I'll just keep telling myself that.

I jump as someone sits down beside me and glance over to find a guy around my age. His dark hair is hidden underneath a baseball cap and his earbuds hang around his neck. I notice a little silver ring in his eyebrow and wonder how painful it was to pierce it there. He glances at me for a second, which gets me all flustered for some reason, and then he sinks low into his seat, keeping his head down and folding his arms.

He obviously doesn't want to talk to anyone. Least of all me. He's way out of my league anyway, so I shouldn't be surprised. Ignoring my new neighbor, I settle into my squishy, yet uncomfortable seat and stare out the window until the plane takes off and we're in the air.

I'm doing the right thing. I'm doing the right thing.

Am I? Am I really?

Please tell me I'm doing the right thing.

CHAPTER 7

In too deep, nowhere to go
Watch my life spiral out of control
You're the one who keeps me here
Locked in this battle with my worst fear
—J.S.

It's been an hour. Maybe two. And honestly, I've never been so bored in my entire life. I guess my history class could count as the most boring thing ever, but I digress. I could at least get up and go to a different class after. When you're stuck on a plane, things don't change. And I can only get up to "go to the bathroom" so many times before people start looking at me funny.

I'm on bathroom visit number three already. And from the old lady sitting across the aisle keeps looking at me, I know she's counting. After another scowl in my direction, she goes back to her knitting and pulls her thick jacket closer around her.

It's like ninety degrees in here.

I squirm in my seat and stare out the little window again, seeing nothing but wispy clouds and flat land below. My stomach lurches at how high we are so I focus on the seat in front of me to take my mind off it. If only I would have brought my Kindle or some music or *something*. I'm an idiot.

The guy next to me has had his earbuds in almost the whole flight so far, but I notice he's taken them out. I fight the temptation to steal them and his MP3 player. It would give me something to do, but probably wouldn't be the smartest move ever. I'm not here to get arrested for stealing. Though the thought of listening to music makes me think it might be worth it. Anything to take my mind off worrying about Madison. Or what my angry parents are doing right now. Or old ladies who like to glare at me. Or the dumb decision not to pack anything to keep me entertained during a cross-country flight. Or that fact that I'm hundreds of feet in the air with only a big slab of metal keeping me from falling to my death.

Pretty sure I'm afraid of heights. Just a little . . .

I startle as the guy next to me suddenly shrugs out of his leather jacket. My eyes are drawn to his bare arms, because . . . Well . . . Who doesn't love nice arms? I try not to stare but can't help looking at the tattoo swirling around his right bicep. Some intricate wrap-around about an inch wide in a sleek design. Not sure if it's meant to be some kind of symbol or just cool to look at. But believe me, it's pretty awesome. It kind of reminds me of one of Dad's, but this guy is . . . uh . . . very nice to look at. He glances over at me and I hurry and pretend I'm interested in something in my purse. After he puts his jacket on the floor, he ignores me completely and grabs a magazine from the little holder on the back of the seat in front of him.

As he sets it in his lap, I stare at the headline, even though I hate when people read over my shoulder. But I can't help it. I'm beyond bored. And I wonder why I didn't pick up the magazine earlier.

BLUE FIRE ON VERGE OF BREAK-UP!
Lead Singer Jaxton Scott ready to call it quits.

I chuckle. "Good. I hate that band." My cheeks redden. I didn't really mean to say that out loud.

The guy glances up, a curious look on his face. "Blue Fire?"

"Yeah." I smile, kind of proud of myself now for starting a conversation with a complete stranger. "I can't stand all the screaming. One, it's annoying. And two, it gives me a headache."

His blue eyes grow wide for a second and then he breaks into an easy smile. "Huh. Interesting." He sets the magazine in the holder again and leans back, his arms folded. "You don't listen to a lot of rock?"

I shrug. "There's a difference between rock and screaming. One requires talent, the other doesn't."

"Really? Enlighten me."

"Okaaaay . . . " I reach forward, grab the magazine, and stare at the four guys on the cover, dressed in black with piercings all over their faces. "These guys are just . . . creepy. And trying to be trendy. Know what I mean?" He raises an eyebrow but doesn't answer, so I continue. "I'm sure they have . . . uh . . . Talent, but I love the old rock. The real rock. Metallica, Zeppelin, AC/DC. The classics."

"Understandable. They have good stuff." He sits back in his seat and slouches down again.

"Right? I'm not a fan of knock-offs. Or trends. I like the real deal. I guess I'm old school?"

"Not a bad thing," he says.

"Thanks. These guys are just a bunch of punks with makeup on. I don't like fake. And they can't get any faker. And the fact that they're always fighting and threatening to break up is annoying, too. If you don't like what you're doing, just quit. Don't be so dramatic about it. But I guess Hollywood is all about the drama. What would we regular people do with ourselves without all the celebrity gossip?" I chuckle. I don't follow Hollywood as much as Maddy does. She loves it all.

He stares at me a second before clearing his throat. "You make it seem like a simple thing to do."

"Huh?" No idea what he's talking about.

"Quit."

"Oh. Well, why wouldn't it be simple? You hate something, so why make yourself miserable?"

A trace of a frown graces his lips before he smiles and looks away. "No idea."

He doesn't say anything else, so I focus on my new entertainment for the moment. I flip through the magazine, curious about the article now. It's not like I listen to Blue Fire, but a good scandalous story is sometimes fun to pass the time.

I scan the article. Apparently, the rumor mill says the lead singer wants to quit, but nothing official has happened yet. Not too surprising. Someone's always threatening to quit a band and then they never do. Or they do quit and then go back to the band a year later saying they'd made a mistake. I'd seen it all before.

Hollywood is a fickle place with nothing but divas in its playground.

The band's pictures are splashed all over the pages. Dark hair, dark makeup, black painted nails. So not my style. There are pictures of them drinking, crowded around by girls in tight short dresses, big smiles, a few of them playing live at some venue.

Why would anyone want that lifestyle? Drinking your life away for what? To be plastered all over the news the next day when you get a DUI or show up to your next show with a hangover from the night before?

Not worth it.

One picture in the left-hand corner catches my attention and I take a closer look. It's of the lead singer, Jaxton. He actually looks normal. And he's doing something normal. Not partying it up in Hollywood. He's taking the trash out of his Hollywood home, no makeup or black clothes at all. He's cute underneath all the layers of crap they put on him to make him some kind of symbol.

His dark hair is spiked and he's wearing basketball shorts and a T-shirt. My eyes are drawn to the tattoo on his right arm. It's sexy. I swear I've seen it before, though.

I stiffen. I grimace and barely stop myself from cursing aloud.

Oh no.

I swallow and glance to my left to find my neighbor staring at me with an amused smile on his face.

Or should I say, I find *Jaxton Scott* staring at me with an amused smile on his face.

Jaxton Scott is sitting next to me. And I just told him his band sucks.

Someone kill me now.

"Um . . ." My mouth goes dry and all I want to do is get up and jump off the plane. Preferably with a parachute. My cheeks heat and I set the magazine in my lap, closing it and smoothing down the crinkles. I sit up a little straighter, take a shaky breath. And clear my throat. "So . . . About that conversation we just had . . ." I trail off and look at him, surprised to find him still smiling. "Blue Fire isn't . . . That bad . . . ?"

I wait for him to demand another seat. To get up and yell at me or shame me in front of all the passengers on the plane. But he does something that surprises me.

He laughs.

I stare at him with my mouth hanging open. "I . . ."

I want to say I'm sorry, but I can't find the right words. And honestly, I don't think he wants to hear me say anything else for the rest of the flight.

He reaches over and puts a finger on my chin to push my mouth closed. "It's okay. I promise I'm not mad. I'll admit I was a little shocked at how animated you were when you were telling me how awful Blue Fire was, but no worries. I appreciate your honesty." He grins and removes his finger from my chin. "You'd make a good critic. I don't think I've ever been ripped that bad in my life. And I even got to experience it firsthand. Very entertaining."

I'm still staring at him. My face is flaming, I'm sure.

A minute or two goes by before he speaks again. "You can talk, you know. I don't bite."

He smiles again and I work to spit out the right words. "Um . . . hi?"

Smooth, Mia. Real smooth.

"I'm Jaxton," he says, holding out his hand.

I hesitate only a second before grabbing it. "Mia. Mia Cox."

"Hello, Mia Cox. It's nice to meet you."

Why the heck did I tell him my last name?

I notice he keeps his voice down and doesn't tell me *his* full name. I'm guessing from the way he's wearing his hat that he doesn't want to be recognized. "So . . ." I start. "You're . . . um . . . kind of a rockstar."

Keep going, Mia. You're doing awesome.

"Well, from the way you just described my band, I'd call myself a trendy *wannabe* rockstar."

My face flames again, and I sink lower in my seat with a groan.

"I'm totally kidding. Don't feel bad."

"I'm an idiot." I put my face in my hands, like it will help hide my shame.

"No, actually, you're not. I liked that you had no idea who I was while you were spouting off your distaste for my music. It was refreshing. You didn't fall all over yourself and compliment me. Or take a billion pictures. Like I said. I like honesty. And I don't like fake people."

I glance up again and smile. "I don't like fake people either. That's why I stay away from Hollywood news. Not that you're fake or anything. Just . . . A lot of people in Hollywood are."

"Well, I'm glad to know we have that in common since we'll be keeping each other company all flight."

A hint of a smile plays at my lips and I blush *again* under his gaze. I still feel so stupid. Maddy never would have done something like this. She would have recognized him the second he sat down in his seat. She'll enjoy this story, for sure. Especially since it has to do with Jaxton Scott. She loves Blue Fire. We tend to agree on most things, but Blue Fire isn't one of them.

"Now that you know how vile I can be, could I ask you a question?"

He raises an eyebrow. "Depends on what you want to ask. Is it vile? Scandalous? Worth reporting?"

I chuckle. "No. You're safe. This time, anyway. I'll be nice, I swear."

"Ask away then."

"What are you doing sitting in coach? Shouldn't you be . . . You know. In first class with the rest of the rich and famous people? Drinking champagne, eating caviar, sleeping on fluffy pillows? All that fun stuff?"

He shrugs. "Most of the time, I'd rather not be noticed."

I smile, not really believing what he's saying. Who wouldn't notice him? I guess I didn't, for a second, but I'm the anomaly. "You're kind of one of those people who other people notice." My eyes nearly pop out of my head when I realize it sounds like I'm hitting on him. *Stop talking, Mia.* "I mean . . . uh . . . people know who you are and stuff."

He leans toward me, a sly grin on his face. "You're pretty noticeable yourself."

I choke out a laugh, which comes out louder than I expected. After glancing around to make sure people aren't staring, I shake my head. "Right."

"That guy over in the next row? He's been staring at you since you boarded."

I don't dare look where he's gesturing. "That's creepy."

"Not like full on staring, but he *has* been checking you out. I wouldn't be surprised if he came over to talk to you." He glances over at the guy, and I try to catch a glimpse of him out of the corner of my eye. When that doesn't work, I turn my head a little more, make eye contact, and chuckle as the guy suddenly gets really interested in the magazine he's holding. "See? He's jealous I'm talking to you right now. And if it were the other way around, I'd be jealous of him."

"Oh, please. Do you use that line often?" He thinks he's so smooth just because he's a rockstar or heartthrob or whatever. I don't know what they call musicians in Hollywood. A Rock God?

He puts a hand to his chest. "Me? Never."

"Not buying it. You're paid to be a flatterer."

"Not right now. All I'm doing is paying you a compliment. I noticed you before I even sat down."

"Mmmm hmmm." I roll my eyes.

"Really. Contrary to what the tabloids say, I'm quite shy. I'm not the type to just start a conversation, so thanks for that. You made things way less awkward than they would have been."

"Are you serious? Because the conversation I started with you couldn't have been any more awkward. I insulted you. Multiple times."

He laughs. "Yet, here I sit."

I frown. "Yes. . . . Here you sit." Weird. I glance around for more band members. He can't be here alone, can he? "Where are your bodyguards? The rest of Blue Fire? Aren't you supposed to travel with a manager or something?"

"No one knows I'm here."

"I'm sure someone does. You have like fifty people who follow you around wherever you go."

"Nope. No one. I'm taking a spontaneous vacation to New York. Indefinitely."

I stare at him. "You're messing with me. You have places to be. People to see. Concerts to . . . Yell at." I grin.

He leans back in his seat with a chuckle. "Not if I can help it."

"No gig you're playing at tomorrow?" Did I really just say *gig*?

He shakes his head.

"No girlfriend or groupies you're surprising after a big tour?"

He snorts.

"I take that as a no . . ."

"No on both accounts." His blue eyes hold mine and I see the truth in them. And something else I can't place yet. "I haven't dated anyone in over a year."

"Oh." It's all I can think to say. I think I remember some blonde girl he dated for a really long time. Maddy would know, since she's obsessed. "Well, that's . . . Awesome?"

He smiles at that. "Is it?"

I scoot away, not sure what he's implying but unable to break eye contact.

"Drinks?"

The stewardess's voice snaps me out of whatever trance I'm in and I glance away from him.

"Water?" I squeak. I clear my throat. "Water would be great."

Jaxton shoots me a small smile. "I'll have the same."

She hands us some mini water bottles. I twist the cap and down mine in two seconds. And I'm not even joking.

"Thirsty?" Jaxton sips his and puts the cap back on before setting it in his drink holder. He looks so relaxed compared to the hot mess I am right now.

"Yes." My mouth is still dry. I'm sure I could down three more bottles. I can't shake the nervousness I've been feeling since I figured out who he is. A rockstar. Who I've insulted several times already but for some reason won't stop talking to me.

Not that I mind. I just didn't expect someone like him to be so down to earth. He's so . . . normal. Maddy should be here instead of me. She'd love this.

"So what's your story then?" He makes himself comfortable in our very uncomfortable seats. "Are you on your way to visit family? Or are you meeting a secret lover somewhere?"

"A secret *what*? No!" I have to think fast. I wasn't really expecting to tell anyone why I'm here. Should I? He's a stranger. He could . . . I don't know. Stalk me or something. "Uh, I'm headed to New York. Same as you. Just sightseeing. I've never been there before and wanted to, uh, see the sights?"

"By yourself?"

"Yep." Ha. A rockstar stalking me. That's probably the stupidest thought I've ever had. I'm sure he has his fair share of stalkers. I glance at him out of the corner of my eye and find him watching me, a curious look on his face. "What? Why are you looking at me like that? I've always wanted to see New York."

He gives me a *I totally know you're lying* look and folds his arms. "I have a feeling there's a story here."

"Nope. No story. Just a girl on a plane who wants to check out the Big Apple. Isn't that everyone's dream anyway? Why else would I be on this plane?"

He smiles. "You can tell me the truth. I'm listening."

CHAPTER 8

Let me go, leave me be,
Rid me of these demons, I want to be free
—J.S.

I don't know what to say to him, and I can't seem to look away from his very blue eyes. I swear they're like the blue sky shining above the clouds. I chuckle to myself. That was so lame. I'd never make it as a poet or a songwriter. I'll stick to the piano.

"Mia?"

I jump as he says my name and snaps me back to reality. *Wow. Jaxton Scott knows my name.*

I distract myself from staring at him like an idiot by flipping through the magazine again. "I don't know you. Why would I tell you personal things when I don't know you?"

"You don't know me?" He laughs. "I'm sure you could find out lots of juicy details in that magazine of yours. Or pull out your phone and look me up. You can find out anything you want."

I glance over at him, trying not to smile. "I don't keep up on famous people like the rest of the world does."

"Really? So you don't believe everything you read? Or hear?"

"Not usually."

"Huh."

I shrug. "Famous people are just that: people."

He smiles, a touch of a dimple in his left cheek. Nothing huge, but you'll see it if you stare like I am. "I wish everyone thought the way you do. That we're just people."

I reach over and jab him in the arm. "See? You're just a person. Like me."

Holy crap, I just touched him again.

"Deep thinker there." He smiles as he jabs me back. "So, focusing on you again. What are you running away from? A crazy ex? Crazy parents? Come on. I'm getting some kind of *crazy* vibe from you." His eyes widen. "Not that you're crazy . . ."

I chuckle at the pink tint in his cheeks, happy to be the one not blushing for once "Crazy does sum up my life right now, I guess." I twist my hands in my lap before looking at him again. "But who says I'm running away from something?"

"I just assumed. Since you kind of avoided my questioning earlier."

"Yeah, I guess I did. But, no. I can assure you I'm not running away from anything at the moment. I'd rather call it running *toward* something."

"Oh? A new life or something?"

I shake my head. "No. Not for me. For my little sister."

He raises an eyebrow, the little silver ring in it looking twice as painful as it crunches into his skin. "Your sister?"

I nod, not sure if I should keep going. But then I realize I'll probably never ever see Jaxton again since we live in two very different worlds, so . . . Why not? And I bet he's not going to bother stalking me.

"You don't have to tell me if you don't want to." He's watching me, but I don't look at him.

"No, it's fine. We're going to go our separate ways anyway when this is all over, right?"

"Yep." He leans toward me, a hint of mint on his breath. "And if it makes you feel any better, I'm good at keeping secrets. It's a talent, really. I swear I'll take it to my grave."

I raise an eyebrow. "Secret-keeping is a talent now?"

"Yes. And believe me when I say I have a lot of secrets to keep because of my career choice. When you're in the spotlight all the time, you have to have some kind of normalcy in your life. Know what I mean?" I nod, even though I haven't the slightest idea of what it feels like for people to know everything about me. "People don't know the real me. They just know the person my band and manager has made. It's all a show." He frowns. "All of it."

For some reason, I have the desire to touch him again. His hand, his arm, something to give him comfort from whatever it is that's eating at him. Because under the smile and his gorgeous blue eyes, there's a darkness there. A sadness, deep in his soul.

But I don't want to pry into his personal life. Instead I move the subject back to me. "My sister's dying."

He glances up, his dark lashes framing his light blue eyes. "What? Why? What happened?"

"Kidney disease. She's in the final stage." I suck in a breath and try to keep the emotion at bay. "That's why I'm here. On this plane and by myself. I wasn't a match to give her one of my kidneys and now our birth mother is her last hope. And, since she lives in New York, I thought I'd track her down. Hopefully."

He sits in silence for a moment, his brow crinkling into a frown. "Isn't there a donor list for kidneys? Is she a good candidate for one?"

"Yeah. She's on it. She's been on it forever, actually. And she'll stay on that stupid list until she dies."

"How do you know?"

I glance at him. "I just do." The sinking feeling I've had all week graces me with its presence right then and I fight it from dragging me down. "There are a lot of people waiting for transplants and not enough people donating. We might get one if we're lucky, but I don't think we're that lucky."

He sits there for a moment, I assume taking in my words. "So, this mom of yours—I take it you're not close?"

I snort. Which is super hot, I'm sure. "I wouldn't go as far as to call her my *mom*, so no. We're not close. How'd you guess?"

He shrugs. "I kind of figured it out since you said 'birth mother.' If you're not calling her 'Mom' then I take it you don't see her very often?"

I laugh. "That would be an understatement. I haven't seen her since I was three. She abandoned us when we were little. And if my dad knew I was on my way to see her right now, he'd flip out. Like seriously."

Oh, Dad. What will you do when you find out I'm gone? The thought of him freaking out and coming after me makes my stomach churn. I wonder if he's called and kind of wish I could turn on my phone. But I don't want to get in trouble. And I really don't want his wrath right now.

"Then why . . ."

I sigh. "Because she's her only hope. She's the most likely person to be a match other than me and my dad."

"Could you have called her? It seems like a lot to fly across the country *by yourself* to see someone you barely know."

I don't miss the way he says "by yourself" but decide it's not worth arguing about the fact that I'm old enough to make my own choices. I'm sure he's made some stupid ones, too. And he seriously can't be much older than I am and he's flying by himself, too.

"That would be an awesome phone call to make. 'Hi Carmen, this is Mia. You know, the three-year-old you abandoned fifteen years ago? Can I have one of your kidneys? To save the other daughter you abandoned? That would be super awesome of you. Thanks so much!'"

He raises his eyebrows. "Okay, you've got a point."

I take a deep breath, surprised at all the mixed emotions I'm feeling, and calm myself down. "It would probably be better to talk to her in person about something as serious as this. Seeing how my sister's life is on the line. Know what I mean?"

"Agreed."

I fold my arms and lean back against my seat. My emotions are dangerously close to the surface. Anger, annoyance, fear. I don't know which one to focus on, so I clear my throat and force a smile. "So, since I spilled everything about myself, what about you? What's your story?" I need to stop worrying about Maddy. I need something else to talk about.

He chuckles and shakes his head. "What do you want to know?"

I study him, wondering what to ask. Maybe I shouldn't start with something serious since he seems pretty hardcore. My eyes fall on the silver ring in his eyebrow again and I clear my throat. "I'm afraid to ask, but . . ." I nod toward his eyebrow ring. "Did it hurt?"

He looks confused for a split second before easing into a grin. "When I fell from Heaven?"

It takes me a second to absorb the lameness of the joke, and then I can't help but burst out laughing. "You did *not* just say that. Please. Tell me you didn't say it."

He laughs, deep and loud, earning us a glare from the older lady across from us. "What? That's not what you were asking?"

"You know what I was asking."

He laughs again. "I know. But really. Do you think there's any chance someone like me fell from Heaven?"

I giggle again. "Stop. Please. I can't handle it. It's like I'm back in middle school with all the puberty-ridden boys and their dumb little pick-up lines. You probably used some, huh?"

He puts his hand over his face. "Don't remind me. Middle school was pretty bad, right?" He chuckles again and stretches his arms over his head before folding them across his chest. "Oh, I haven't laughed like that for a while. Thanks for that."

"You're the one that said it. I'd never think of something that . . ."

"Stupid?"

"Yes. Exactly. I'm all about . . ." I can't think of a word. "Sophisticated conversations?"

"Okay, this is when I leave . . ." He pretends to get out of his seat and I grab his arm and pull him back down.

"I'm joking." We both laugh again. I'm surprised at how easy it is to talk to him. It's . . . Weird, but oddly comforting at the same time. Maddy will love him even more when I tell her about him. "So, tell me about the piercing."

He shrugs. "Got it about two years ago." He reaches up, fingering the little loop. "It hurt at first, but wasn't a big deal." He nudges my shoulder. "But I'm supposed to be a tough guy, so take that for what you will."

"Interesting. I have my ears pierced, but nothing else. I'm too chicken."

"Eh. I'm debating on taking this out for good. We did it as a band. Kind of a spontaneous thing after a concert one night. I'm getting a little sick of it."

I'm not sure if he's talking about the band or his piercing, so I give him a little nudge to keep talking. "So, why are you running away? I'm guessing it has to do with band stuff, since you know—the magazine articles are *so* right about everything."

"Ha. Right." He winks.

"But really. Since I spilled everything it's only fair to hear your story now."

"It's a long story."

"We have two hours until our lay-over, which gives us another hour after that to get on the next plane. If we're on the same plane." I realize this may not be the case and pull out my ticket to check the flight.

He looks at it, too. "Yep. Same plane."

"Great, so no getting out of this. I'm pretty sure I have time to listen to you for that long. It's not like I can get up and leave." I glance around. "I guess I can get up and go *somewhere*, but the places I can hide out are numbered."

He smiles and glances around as well. "Nothing like being trapped on an airplane hundreds of feet in the air, huh?"

"Ugh. Don't remind me."

"Sorry. Didn't think you were afraid of heights."

"I'm not. Just . . . not super thrilled about them."

He's quiet a moment and looks like he's going to start his story, but he hesitates. "I'm not sure what to tell you, Mia. After hearing your story, mine will just sound stupid."

"What do you mean?"

"You're trying to save your sister. You're doing something totally out of your comfort zone because you love her. That says a lot about your character already and I barely know you."

"But—"

"You're selfless." He smiles. "Don't worry. It's a good thing."

I don't know what to say, and with his gaze on me, all I can do is stare. I swallow, hard and look away.

"Then there's me. The screw-up who's running away from his life." He looks at his hands then links them together before putting them in his lap.

I focus my attention back to the magazine on my own lap. I pick it up and point at his picture. "So the magazine stories. What should I believe?"

"None. Well, some are true. To a point." He rubs his hand over his face, and I notice the black fingernail polish on his nails is chipped in several places. He catches me staring again and laughs. "See? Dumb. I hate fingernail polish."

"Me too." Which is totally a lie. I freaking love it. I glance at my light blue fingernails and notice a little spot came off my pinky. Sad. I frown and rub at it with a finger.

He gives me half a smile as he notices. "Busted."

"Yeah . . . I sort of like it. "

He smiles again.

"Okay, fine. I love it. I probably have around fifty bottles of fingernail polish sitting in my bottom dresser drawer at home." I frown, thinking of all those colors back home. I wish I had thought to bring some with me. "I could totally give you the manicure of your life if we were there. I don't do feet, though. Gross. Besides my own."

He laughs and leans his head back against his seat.

62

I rub the goosebumps on my arms and lean back, too. The air finally turned on, so it's pleasant and cool. "So, what's your story then?"

"Get ready to be bored out of your mind." He grins.

Whatever. There is no way this is gonna be boring.

CHAPTER 9

You look at me with your deep brown eyes
You take away the secrets and lies
All I need is you next to me
To be the man I wish to be
—J.S.

"When I started this gig, I thought it was a once in a lifetime opportunity to get my music out there. To actually hear it playing on the radio and streaming online. Hold my own CD in my hand. But with it comes other things. I never wanted all this." He gestures to the magazine.

"Fame?"

He shrugs. "Yeah."

"Then why . . ."

"I love music."

"So do I?" I raise an eyebrow, not sure where the conversation is going.

He smiles, his dimple showing again. "I'm probably confusing you more than making you understand, right?"

"Keep going and I'll try to keep up."

"Okay. Let's start at the beginning."

I nod as a song pops in my head. "A very good place to start."

"Ha. That's my Mom's favorite movie."

"You know what that's from?"

"Of course I do. *The Sound of Music* is a classic."

Holy crap. I think I'm in love. "Anyway, sorry to interrupt."

"You're fine." He sinks lower in his seat and I do the same. "So, when I was in high school, I was in a band."

"High school as in . . . A long time ago?" I'm curious how old he is.

"I graduated last year."

Interesting. "I start my senior year in a few weeks. My parents held me back a year because they didn't want me to be the youngest in my class." I frown. I could totally have graduated by now if they hadn't done that. "Anyway. Sorry. Continue."

"Right. So, we hooked up as freshmen and played everywhere. We were good. Real good. Good enough that we sent in our mix to a record company at the end of our junior year and they signed us that month."

"That's amazing."

"Yeah, it was pretty cool. Anyway, we played a few gigs just to test the waters and got a great reception. So, we started touring. I finished my senior year on the road, which was hard, but doable. Now, we had been friends for years. And touring together for two years was fun, but exhausting. And then there's the fame that comes with it,

65

and you know. It kind of goes to your head. Which is what happened—"

"To you?"

He chuckles. "No. My drummer. And my bassist. And my guitarist."

"Don't you play the guitar, too?"

"Yes."

"Awesome." Love a man that plays the guitar. I mean . . . like, not love. It's sexy. But I'm not about to tell him that.

"Parties, gigs, tours, huge venues almost every night. It's too much. You wouldn't believe how little sleep I've gotten the past few years. And when you're on the road so much, you'll do anything for a little sleep. And sleep anywhere too." He shivers as though he's thinking of some unpleasant memory. "Basically it all catches up to you. Partying, no sleeping, partying some more. Pushing your body to the limit isn't good." He rubs at his eyes. "All the makeup, the changes they've put us through. Things they've made us do. It's just too much." He laughs. "You know, all I want to do is write music. I don't care about all that . . ." He glances around and sees the old woman with the heavy coat on scowling at him. "Crap."

I can't help but laugh at his word choice. Ten points for being a gentleman. "So the black clothes and stuff wasn't your idea I'm guessing?"

"Ha."

"Interesting. So, is the screaming your idea of music then? Or did they make you do that, too?"

He shrugs. "If they want you to sound a certain way, you have to comply. I just write the lyrics and the music. I don't scream in all the songs, but a lot of them."

"Huh."

"Huh? That's all?"

"That's got to be hard on your voice."

"Sometimes it is. Especially if we play several nights in a row."

"I don't get it."

"What don't you get?"

"I just . . . I don't get why they won't let you do what you want. It's dumb."

He sits up straighter. "They make you do what sells."

"Well, that's stupid. If you hate it so much, why do you still do it? If you don't love what you're doing, it's not worth it. I play the piano, but I pick and choose what I play. No one tells me what I *have* to play. I mean, when I was little, my teacher told me what to play, of course, because I was just learning, but now, I play what I love."

"That's different, though."

"Is it?" I stare at him with what I hope is a challenging look on my face.

"Yes. You play what you want to play because you're not tied down to a contract or anything. But if you want to do something else, like make a CD or something, you'll have to play by the record label's rules."

He's got a point I guess. "Why *do* you do it then?"

"I ask myself that question every day. That's one of the reasons I'm on this plane." He laughs as he says it. Not a happy laugh, just a pity laugh. "I don't want to do it anymore. I don't want to be famous. I want to be . . . normal. You know?"

"Kind of hard when you're in so deep, though. Because you are. In deep."

He sighs. "I know. That's why it's complicated."

I nod, not knowing what to say.

"So, there's my big secret. It's stupid and selfish, but what can you do?"

"I wouldn't call it selfish. You're doing what you want to do for a change. Not what someone's telling you to do."

"Trying to." He pulls out his phone, looks at it for a second, and puts it back in his pocket. "I keep thinking someone's going to call, but I turned it off." He smiles. "I'm never not expecting a phone call."

"Yeah, Totally opposite of me. I don't expect many calls. Like, ever."

He laughs. "That would be nice."

"So, you're going to quit? Just like that?"

"Not that simple. I really hate the fact that people tell me what to write, what to sing. But I could get in huge trouble, I have a contract. Running away isn't the answer. I can't run away. But I thought it would be good to get away for a while anyway. Take a little break."

I lift my hand, hesitating only a second before placing it on his arm. "You'll figure things out. I know it."

"I hope."

His skin is warm and my fingers shake a bit from my stupid nerves, so I put my hand back in my lap. "So, where are you running to?"

"Home."

"Like a home you own? Yourself?"

"No. My family has a place on Long Island. It's nice."

"Cool." I'm pretty sure Long Island is where The Statue of Liberty is. Maybe. I should know my states and cities better. I need to pay more attention at school.

"You've never been to New York, have you?"

"Is it that obvious?"

He grins. "No. Just a lucky guess."

"Good. I think. I've been lots of other places, if that counts."

"Like?"

Crap. "Um, I went to Washington once. To visit my uncle."

"Washington's nice. Lots of rain."

"Yes. It does rain a lot." I frown. I bet he's been to every state in the United States. "I've been to Las Vegas."

"Nevada. That's two. Three if you count California."

"Yes. Three. And I've been to Utah to visit my cousin, Cole. So four states in all. Holy frick, I'm a loser."

"Not a loser. Just not a traveler. Nothing wrong with that."

"I'd love to travel someday."

"It's fun. Sometimes."

I pick at the little spot on my pinky nail and watch as blue paint flecks fall to the floor. I'm going to have to repaint this nail anyway, so I might as well get it all off. "So," I start. "What's your favorite state you've been to? Or place? I'm sure you've been out of the country."

He nods. "I'm a big fan of Florida. Nice beaches. The Everglades are cool."

"I've always wanted to go there."

"You should. It's awesome. I like being warm. Although it is a bit too humid for me. I can't do a thing with my hair."

I glance at him and he grins. "Right. Hair probs. I can relate."

He chuckles. "But for real, it's humid. Right when I walk outside it feels like I've been sweating for hours. It's kind of like when you get out of the shower and the room's filled with steam and you can't get dry no matter how hard you try."

"Like a sauna?"

He laughs lightly and shakes his head. "Yes. That would be what I was trying to describe. A sauna."

"Not a fan of those. I don't like sweat. Did you like any other places you've visited?"

"I loved Hawaii. I wasn't a big fan of being surrounded by ocean, though."

I laugh. "Yeah, that's kind of daunting, isn't it?"

"You never know when the ocean will want it back."

"I know, right?"

"Let's see." He thinks for a moment. "I really liked England. I love history, so the castles and things were cool."

"Oh, England. That's on my bucket list for sure. And Italy." Maddy and I are already planning a trip. She's been begging Mom and Dad to go there for years. If she ever gets better, of course. And she will. She'll get better.

"You'd love Rome. It's amazing. But there's the ocean problem again. At least while you're flying to get to Europe."

"Ugh. I'd probably throw up if we were flying over a whole ocean. I don't know why that's terrifying, but it is."

"Just wear those little orange arm floaties and you'll be prepared in case of an emergency."

"Oh, yeah. Sexy." I chuckle and glance out the window to examine the mountains and green foliage covering the landscape below. "Speaking of flying, where do you think we are?"

He leans over me to look outside, his shoulder brushing mine. "Hmmm . . . I'd guess—"

A woman's voice sounds through the speakers above, making us both jump. "We are approaching the Denver airport. If you could stay in your seats and buckle up, that would be great."

"That was . . ."

"Weird?" he finishes.

"Yes. So will we be spending our layover together?"

"Of course," he says, smiling. "I'd be bored out of my mind if we didn't." He's still leaning across me, looking out the window. He glances at me out of the corner of his eye, a smirk on his face. As he leans back into his seat, his arm bumps mine, making my heart go crazy. I can't figure out why I'm reacting this way. I don't even know the guy. If I get this crazy over someone I just met, I can't imagine what I'll feel like with someone I'm actually dating.

I've never had time to date, though. Not when Maddy can't enjoy dating, too. I have a few good friends I hang out with sometimes—one in particular named Tru—but with all the time I spend with Maddy, it's hard to have a normal high school life.

Speaking of Tru, I should have texted her before I left.

The plane descends and I take out my ticket to get on my next flight. "Hopefully you know where our next gate is because I'd be running around like a crazy person trying to find the right one. Because . . . let's face it. I'm a crazy."

"Trust me. I've seen crazier. And I've been in this airport plenty of times. You'll be fine. Just stick with me." He gives me a reassuring smile and I feel a blush creep to my cheeks. He probably thinks my cheeks are permanently pink at this point.

I'll definitely be sticking with him, though. I glance at my ticket again. "Two-hour layover. That's not too horrible." I say it like I've flown a thousand times. When in reality, I've only flown to Washington. Once.

"Yep. One hour isn't long enough sometimes and more than two is enough to make you bored out of your mind. Two hours is perfect."

As the plane rolls to a stop and the stewardess gives us instructions to exit the plane, the passengers start to stand and get their things. Jaxton turns to me as he stands. "Do you have anything in the overhead?"

"My backpack."

He nods, pulls it out, and motions for me to go in front of him.

"I can take it. You don't have to carry it for me." I try to take it from him, but he just laughs.

"I've got it. You'd better start walking. You're holding up the line." He chuckles as I turn to face a bunch of empty seats. I hear someone grumble about the girl with the dark hair not moving fast enough and practically run down the aisle and into the jetway.

We pass through the gate and I walk over to the window overlooking the airport. "I've never been to Denver. But you probably knew that since I've only been to four states."

Jaxton's shoulder bumps into mine. He has my backpack slung over one shoulder and looks totally relaxed. "Five now."

"Layovers don't count."

"I guess you're right. Denver's nice, though."

"You've been everywhere," I say, watching another plane take off.

"There's no place better than home."

I look over at him, his baseball cap pulled low as he stares out the window, my backpack hitched over his shoulder. "You don't have any luggage?"

He laughs. "No. I didn't need to travel with anything this time. I left pretty quick. Grabbed the last flight, I think."

"Oh."

"I'm going to see my family. They have enough of my stuff there that I don't really need anything but my phone."

"Charger?" I raise an eyebrow.

"Pretty sure I can find a spare charger. Do you know anyone who *doesn't* have a cell phone?"

I shake my head. He's got me there.

"And I have a credit card, of course. Speaking of—you hungry?"

My stomach growls in response.

He leans toward me. "I take that as a yes." He nudges me with his elbow. "Come on. Let's get something to eat before we're stuck on the next flight."

"Okay, but I'm paying."

He doesn't say anything, just throws back his head and laughs in response.

CHAPTER 10

We're heading for something good
That much I know is true
Tell me what you need from me
I'll do anything for you
—J.S.

I'm standing in front of the bathroom mirror, cursing my hair and the mascara smudges under my eyes. Did I really look this bad the entire two hours on the plane? I don't remember looking in the mirror before jumping in my car and heading to the airport. So of course I look my absolute best . . .

After I comb my fingers through my hair and wipe the smudges from under my eyes, it helps, a little. I look tired, though.

I *feel* tired.

I'm doing this for Maddy, though. I'm going to find our mom, ask her to come back home with me, and she will save Maddy's life.

No distractions.

Even if the distraction is a rock-and-roll star. I run my fingers through my hair one more time and sigh.

"This is as good as it's gonna get," I whisper to myself, ignoring the weird look the lady a few sinks over gives me. And then my stomach growls so loud I'm sure everyone in the bathroom can hear it, so I head back out to meet Jaxton.

At least I'll have someone to talk to until I get to New York.

He's standing against the wall reading another magazine. A beautiful man reading is always nice. It just makes them seem so . . . intellectual. I laugh at my random thought and resist the urge to take a picture of him and put him on some website called "Hot guys reading." I'm sure I can find one. Actually, I'm pretty sure it already exists . . .

And it's not like he's not already plastered on every website already. He wouldn't mind, right?

Jaxton lowers the magazine and smiles when he sees me. "So, what do you want for lunch?" He sets the magazine down on one of the chairs by the wall and we head toward the smell of food. "Not much to choose from here. Hope that's okay."

"Well, it's not like we're out on the town." I smile up at him. "I'm sure you could demand some gourmet food and they'd bring it to you in two seconds though. Considering who you are. You know. Play it up. Get rid of the nice-guy persona and pretend you're a Hollywood starlet or something."

He grins. "That would be interesting, wouldn't it?"

"I haven't known you for too long, but I couldn't see you doing that."

"I'm a good actor when I have to be."

My eyes widen. I wonder if he's secretly a diva and actually does demand ridiculous stuff. I breathe a sigh of relief as he chuckles at my expression. "You're joking."

"Of course." We both laugh as we turn the corner, I glance around at the few places to eat. "A hamburger sounds good I think. It's safe."

"Safe?" He stops walking and looks down at me, a question in his eyes and an amused smile.

All I can do is shrug. "What can I say? I don't like surprises."

He chuckles next to me and puts his hands in his pockets. "Surprises? Like what? Tomatoes or pickles?"

"No, those are good. Onions are gross, though. They're nasty little surprises that show up even if you tell them to take them off sometimes. Gag."

"So, onions are not a safe food."

"Correct."

"Noted. You're hilarious, you know that?" He grins and steps up to the counter to order. "A hamburger with pickles and tomatoes it is then. With cheese?"

"Always."

"Ah. A girl who knows a good burger when she sees one. Would you like fries with that?"

"Who doesn't order fries?"

He stares at me, his mouth breaking into a sly grin. "Seriously? I'm considering marrying you right here and right now."

"In a fast food place?"

77

"Why not? A girl who can eat equals the girl of my dreams."

"A fast-food wedding. What could be more romantic than that?" I smile as he puts an arm around my shoulder and squeezes me once before letting go.

I shove my hands in my pockets and try to stop my heart from beating out of my chest.

Jaxton orders our food then and even though I insist on paying, he just shakes his head and laughs. Again.

We sit down at a table for two in the far corner. I watch how he looks around, keeping his head down and hunching over so no one notices him. "I think we're good," I say, gesturing to the empty tables around us.

"You'd be surprised." He unwraps his hamburger. "People recognize me in the least conspicuous places." He takes a bite and chews slowly, still glancing around like someone's going to jump out at us at any moment.

"An airport is pretty conspicuous." Maddy would totally pick him out of a crowd.

He smiles. "You're right. Which is why I look like this and we're sitting by ourselves."

"Do you have a lot of, you know, hardcore fans?"

I say it as he takes a drink and he sort of chokes on it as he laughs. "That would be a yes. A lot of people love Blue Fire. My guitarist, Eric, has his share of fans, and so does my bassist and drummer, but for some reason people focus on the lead singer most of the time. So . . . Yeah. I have a lot of hardcore fans out there. Which can be good and bad."

"Any stalkers?"

The corner of his mouth twitches. "A few." He pops a few fries in his mouth. "No one too crazy, but I do have a restraining order on one girl. She was a nut job."

"Nice."

"She would wait by the corner on my street every day and follow me in her car. Every day. She approached me once, told me we were destined to get married and she wanted to have my babies."

"Wow. Classy."

He laughs. "Classy? Try scary."

"Seriously. I can't imagine people throwing themselves at me. It's got to get old after a while."

"A little." He winks.

We sit in comfortable silence as we finish our meals and I can't help but wonder how the heck I'm even sitting here with him. He's famous. And good looking. More so than I thought I'd ever admit. And . . . nicer than I ever imagined. Not that I've ever imagined much about him before. But he's a good mini distraction to keep my mind off the daunting task of finding Carmen once I reach New York. I should have a better plan, but the truth is, I don't. I have no idea where Carmen lives and have no idea how to get there. I have two addresses, but how can I find said addresses without knowing where anything is? GPS will work, but it's still scary traveling through such a huge city. I need to make a plan soon, and since the adrenaline of actually jumping on a plane heading somewhere I've never been is wearing off, now all I can do is worry. I'll worry less once I'm in the air and actually make a game plan that makes sense.

I'm glad Jaxton is helping me pass the time by talking to me, though. He just seems like a normal guy. Nothing like the stories or the pictures. That must be hard. Seeing so many lies about you and not being able to do anything about it.

As I finish off my water, I notice a girl out of the corner of my eye staring in our direction. She pulls out her phone and points it toward us, obviously snapping a picture. Jaxton notices, too, and shrinks in his seat with a smile on his face, pulling his hat down. "Told you."

My mouth drops open. "People just randomly take pictures of you? Just like that?"

"Yeah. Awesome, right? And I'm sure that one had me chewing a mouthful of food. Can't wait to see that all over the Internet tonight."

I glance over at the girl again; she's being very loud and animated with her friends. They look over at us, too, whispering to each other and giggling. I wait for one of them to walk over, but they never do. "That's so bizarre."

"What?"

"That people just . . . do that. You could be doing anything and they'd just snap a picture without a second thought. It's so . . . I don't know. The whole privacy thing is nonexistent, isn't it?"

"Unfortunately. I'll bet you ten bucks we find that picture online in the next hour."

"Really?" I'm not sure how I feel about my picture

being online. Especially with a celebrity. That would be weird. I guess as long as they don't know my name, right? And if anyone would see it, it would be Maddy.

I pray she won't look online for a few days but expect a phone call just the same.

"Excuse me," someone says.

Jaxton and I both look over at the girl, who now stands with two of her friends next to the table. She runs her fingers through her blond hair and blushes as Jaxton meets her gaze. "Hi," he says, putting on a winning smile.

"You're Jaxton Scott, right?" The girl's voice raises an octave as she says his name.

"Yep. That would be me. And you are?"

"Megan." She squeaks as he reaches out and shakes her hand.

"It's nice to meet you, Megan." He turns toward the next girl and shakes her hand as well.

"I'm Kelly, and this is Leesie," the brunette on the right says. They're all wearing super short shorts and tank tops with their chests busting out of them.

Of course they are. What better fans could Jaxton have than a bunch of gorgeous girls with beach bodies?

I'm not jealous. No, I'm not. I sit back in my seat and fold my arms and watch everything play out.

"Nice to meet you all," Jaxton says.

Megan glances at her friends and giggles. "We were wondering if we could get a picture with you. Is that okay? Oh, and could you sign my cell phone? I think I have a Sharpie in my purse."

Who the heck walks around with Sharpies in their purses?

Instead of being a jerk and dismissing them, Jaxton smiles, stands, and says, "Sure."

The girl, *Megan*, looks at me, a little embarrassed. "Can you take it please? Would you mind?"

I sit up as she puts the phone in my outstretched hand. "I'd be happy to."

She smiles. "The camera is all ready, just tap the screen."

"Okay."

Jaxton stands in the middle as Megan and the two other girls wrap their arms around him. They honestly remind me of how girls in Hollywood would be. Like his groupies or something. He stands there, his arms around them, and they all beam at the camera. I catch myself staring at him through the phone. He's really photogenic, I decide.

Photogenic? Really? What kind of crap thought is that? He just knows how to capture a camera's attention. And every girl's in the airport, as well.

I guess that would be photogenic, right?

Once I've taken a few pictures, Megan comes back and takes her phone. "Thank you." She barely glances at me after that. Instead, she swooshes her hair over her shoulder and touches Jaxton's arm. "It was so nice to meet you, Jaxton."

"You too," he says as he settles down in his seat again. He watches them walk away giggling and scrolling through the pictures on her phone and then shoots me a look. "See? Told you people recognize me everywhere."

"I can see that." I study my fries, not sure if I'm up to eating them. My stomach's a little uneasy for some reason. "You handled it very well, though. You were very smooth."

"Thanks, I think."

I laugh and finish my water. "I meant you were very kind. You didn't treat them like they were beneath you. You know?"

"They're not. Like you said on the plane: I'm a person just like you." He sits there a second, his eyes searching mine, and I watch as he pulls a little notebook and pen out of his pocket. He scribbles a few words down, stares at it for a moment, and smiles at me before sticking both of them in his pocket.

"Writing a song?"

He nods. "I always have lyrics come to me at the most random times."

"Like sitting at lunch in an airport with a complete stranger?"

He chuckles. "This is one of the better times."

I smile at that. "Thanks. Do you always have that notebook with you?"

"Always. This is the fifth one I've gone through."

"That's so cool."

"Not really, but thanks. You ready to find our gate?"

I pile my wrappers on the tray and he picks it up as he stands. "Yep. Lead on. Since you're an airport expert and all."

"You've got that right."

CHAPTER 11

So many words, so little said
—J.S.

We're sitting in front of our gate waiting for our rows of seats to be called when Jaxton pulls out his ticket and glances at it a moment before reaching toward mine. "May I?"

"Sure."

He takes it from me and after looking at it a moment, frowns. "Well, that's a pisser. We're not sitting by each other anymore."

I swear my whole body deflates. "Really?" Seriously. I'm super bummed now. I've kind of liked getting to know my secret rockstar friend. Even if I hate his music.

"Yeah. Not gonna lie. This sucks." We both stand as they call our seats. He's still holding my backpack as he glances at me. "Don't worry. I'll figure something out."

"You really want to sit by me that bad?" I stare at him, my mouth curving into a small smile. I'm flattered. Very.

"Of course. I was looking forward to making you listen to some of my music." He hands the ticket lady his ticket and I notice how she looks right at him, back at his ticket, and then at him again. Her whole personality changes. She flips her red hair over her shoulder. "Welcome aboard, Mr. Scott. Have a nice flight."

"Thank you." He shoots me a look as she studies him closer and he starts to walk away but the ticket lady pulls out her phone. "Wait!"

He turns around, a relaxed smile on his face. "Do you need something else?"

"You're Jaxton Scott. Jaxton Scott, the lead singer of Blue Fire."

He smiles, but looks around. I can see the nervousness coming off him in waves. He pulls his baseball cap down further and gives a small nod.

"Holy—I can't believe it's you! Can I get a picture with you?" She glances around, her eyes falling on the only person standing close enough. Lucky me. Of course. She shoves her phone in my hands and I'm so shocked that I don't move until she snaps at me to take the picture.

"Sorry," I mumble. She's doing an awesome job at being a ticket lady. I kind of want to tell her boss about her. Just to let him know how seriously she takes her job. Especially when a passenger obviously doesn't want to be recognized.

I take a step closer to get them in the shot and focus on their waists up. She totally has her arm around him and he just stands there, calm, collected, and nice as can be. Like he's done it a million times before. Which he probably has. I take the picture and give her phone back to her.

"I'm such a big fan, Jaxton. Such a fan. Thank you so much for the picture. Do you need anything before you board? I could switch you to first class if you'd like. I'm sure I could find a spare seat."

"No, no. That won't be necessary." He reaches a hand toward me and I hesitate only a second before taking it. He pulls me next to him and the lady looks between us a few times before morphing into her professional self again. She takes my ticket and hands it back to me just as fast. "Enjoy your flight, Miss." She clears her throat, her eyes lingering on Jaxton once more before she turns to the next passenger.

"Thanks."

Jaxton still has a hold of my hand and leads me down the jetway. I know he's holding it just to get that lady off his back, but my brain has to concentrate really hard to make my legs work. I feel tingly all over. "That was awkward." He sounds tired. "I just hope she doesn't tell anyone else I'm on here. Since half the passengers out there heard her, I'm sure."

"Yeah. I can only take so many pictures. It's getting old already." I let out an exaggerated sigh.

He chuckles and pulls his cap down over his eyes.

I let go of his hand, even though I really don't want to, and reach up to flick the brim of his hat with my finger. "Can that thing go any lower?"

He shrugs. "Maybe." He pulls it down again, his blue eyes shining as he glances at me.

"Well, I guess this is where we split up," I say, stepping into the plane.

"Not necessarily. I told you I'd figure something out. I'm taking this as a challenge."

"Whatever you say."

The stewardess takes my ticket and points out my seat. I'm in an aisle seat this time. And Jaxton is two rows behind me in the middle.

Boo.

I put my bag in the overhead like last time and sit in my seat, just as a big guy who smells like Fritos points to the seat next to me. I stand, my back pressed into the seat, as he wiggles by me and plops down into his.

"Hi," I try, just to be nice.

He doesn't say a word. He just grabs the barf bag in front of him before he buckles himself tight in his seat.

Great. I'm stuck next to a barfer. Never a good sign.

I pull my phone out and check for missed calls before I turn it off for the flight. Nothing from Mom or Dad yet. I know it's only a matter of time, though. I debate on sending Maddy a text to tell her I'm okay, and assure her I'm not doing anything too stupid, but I don't want Dad to see it and have that get her in trouble, so I put my phone away.

I hope she's okay.

"Hey, Mia. Are you comfortable way up there? Can I get you anything?"

I smile and look behind me. Jaxton's sitting next to some older guy and has a huge grin on his face. "I'm good, I think. Thanks, though!"

"Well, let me know if you need anything."

"Okay." I turn back around, not bothering to hide the smile on my face.

"It's too bad they split us up, huh?" he yells.

My face flames and I sink down in my seat. Why the heck is he talking so loud? Doesn't he know everyone on this plane can hear him? I glance around and notice several people staring at him. "Yep," I say as the Frito guy shifts around in his seat next to me. I'm hoping he's not going to barf before we even take off. That would be fun.

Two seconds later, I swear, someone's tapping me on the shoulder. I look up to see the man who was sitting by Jaxton standing in the middle of the aisle, his bag in his hand. "Hello, young lady. I'd be happy to trade you seats for the flight."

I'm so shocked I can't form a coherent thought. "What?"

"I wanted to trade you seats for the flight so you can sit by your fella back there."

"My . . . You don't have to do that. It's really not a big deal."

He smiles and gestures toward Jaxton. "I insist." He gestures to the aisle and I hurry and unbuckle.

"Well, if you insist. Thank you so much!" I grab my bag and purse and scramble to my new seat. I debate warning the older man about Mr. Frito and the barf bag but figure he'll see it sooner or later. As I make my way back to my new seat, I get a glimpse of Jaxton's face. He's beaming.

After getting my stuff situated, I sit. "So . . . I guess you're stuck sitting by me again. How did you manage to talk that guy into switching seats? Did you bribe him or something? Give him an autograph? Sign a CD?"

He shrugs. "I told him we're on our way to New York to celebrate our first anniversary."

He what? "You told him we were married?" My cheeks heat as my voice raises and he puts a finger to his smiling lips.

"Not quite. I told him we're high school sweethearts and that you're terrified of flying."

That makes me feel a little better. Just a little, though. "Oh. Well, I guess you're sort of right." I lean back against my seat as he laughs and I'm afraid to look at him for some reason.

"You're really that scared of flying?"

"I'm fine."

"I used to get a little nervous, but I've been on so many planes now that it doesn't bother me anymore."

"Thanks for being concerned for my well-being. You must have really wanted to sit by me."

He chuckles. "Obviously."

"Is there a specific reason? I promise I'm not that cool."

He dangles his earbuds in front of my face. "I'm going to attempt to turn you over to the dark side."

"Oh. That."

"Yeah, you're excited. I can tell. You ready?"

It's going to be a long flight.

CHAPTER 12

These demons shift through my troubled soul
They won't relent, they won't let go
I try to make them leave me be
But the one who invited them in, was me
—J.S.

I take the earbuds and smirk at him. "You have your own albums on your MP3 player?"

"What's wrong with that?"

"It's a little weird."

"You can't tell me if you had a CD or something out in the world that came from deep inside your soul, you wouldn't have a copy of it."

"Well . . . When you put it that way." I think of maybe having a piano album someday. That would be cool. And honestly, I'd probably have posters of it hanging around my room and a stack of them displayed on my dresser.

Yeah, I'd be just like him. Probably worse.

He gives me an *I told you so* smile. "It's not like I listen to it all the time. Sometimes I do before a show, just in case I need to hear a guitar solo or need to refresh my memory on an old song, but mostly it's just there for . . . I don't know. *Your* enjoyment perhaps?"

I sigh and stick the earbuds in my ears while he scrolls through his player and pushes a few buttons. Music blasts in my ears and I grab the player out of his hand to turn it down. "Are you losing your hearing? Because seriously? Mine's gone now."

He puts his fingers to his lips to tell me I'm talking way too loud and I shrink down in my seat as I see all the people staring in my direction. Oops.

The music softens and, at first, I don't want to listen to it anymore. I'm a classics kind of girl. I don't like this stuff. But as I keep listening, feeling the rhythm and really letting the music seep into me, something changes. It's not as bad as I was expecting it to be. I mean, I've heard a few of their songs, but refused to really listen to them because I didn't want to get caught up in what everyone else was listening to. But I have to admit, I'm impressed. Even if I can't really focus on the lyrics right now.

Jaxton is watching me and gives me a hopeful thumb's up. I overexaggerate a sigh and give him a slight nod.

He beams.

After I've gone through several songs, I pull my left earbud out so I can talk to him while I listen to the music. It feels weird sitting next to him while he's waiting for me to finish the album. "So . . . I take back most of what I said. Your stuff is pretty good. And I'm not just saying that because you've been so nice to me. It really is good. The guitars, the bass, the drums. It's awesome. How many of these did you write?"

"Most."

"Which ones didn't you write?"

"The trendy ones." He grins. "Did you listen to the lyrics at all?"

I shrug. "I don't listen to lyrics on purpose. The music is what gets me. Sometimes I subconsciously memorize lyrics though and don't realize I'm jamming out to a dirty song until I bust the words out. Which is usually very unfortunate." Oh, the times I could take back. Especially when my little brother was in the car.

"Music is amazing, but lyrics are from the soul. They're the heart of the song." He frowns. "At least most of the time. Sometimes they're just plain weird."

"Agreed."

"So, what kind of stuff do you play on the piano?"

"All kinds of stuff. Mostly the greats. Beethoven, Bach. Mozart. Chopin. Vivaldi is one of my favorites."

"'Four Seasons'?"

"You know it?"

He shrugs. "Who doesn't?"

Seriously. Is this guy for real? After staring at him for a second, I shake my head to bring my thoughts to a safer place and continue. "Anyway . . . classics. Yeah. Love them."

"How long have you been playing?"

"Since I was a little girl. Four or five maybe?"

He nods and smiles as if remembering a pleasant

memory. "I started guitar when I was six. Have you played anywhere?"

I shrug. "Mostly accompanying people singing, but I did solos for Festival at school."

"And?"

I shrug. "I got superiors three years in a row."

He holds his fist out and we bump. "Nice."

He picks at his dark fingernails. "So, when you sit down to play, what's your favorite part of the piece? The climax? The end?"

"I love preludes. Whether they're the beginning of the song or the introduction to a new movement in a complex piece. I like waiting for what comes next. To see how drastic the change between pieces are. Weird, I know."

"The prelude to any piece of music is the most important part of a song, I think. It has to be distinct. Different than everything else out there. It's like the hook. Or the tease before the masterpiece, if you will."

"Ooooh . . . I like that. I really like that." No wonder he's a songwriter. He definitely has a way with words.

"I just made it up right now. Sometimes I like to think I'm awesome."

"Well, I'm glad someone does." I chuckle. "I love interludes, as well. Not really the wedding and church interludes, but the interlude in the middle of a pop or rock song. Like a real nice guitar solo to take you away from the lyrics for a bit. It's nice."

"I still think you should do yourself a favor and focus

on the lyrics of some songs. They're just as good, if not better than, the music itself."

I chuckle at that and hand the left earbud to him as I scroll through his MP3 player. "I'll keep that in mind." Maybe. "So this is the kind of stuff I listen to." I click on a popular band from the nineties and he nods as the music blasts in our ears.

"Yes. Great stuff. I can see why you have a hard time with Blue Fire."

"It's different from my norm, I'll admit, but really, it wasn't as bad as I thought it was going to be." He raises an eyebrow and I need to turn his attention elsewhere. "Oh, this drum solo is amazing. Love it."

"It's funny what kind of stuff you listen to when you play the piano and like the classical stuff so much. There are a lot of bands you've paused on that are totally opposite."

I shrug. "I like variety. There are some interesting bands on your playlist, as well, but who am I to judge?"

"True." He smiles as he bobs his head to the beat until the song ends and then pulls the earbud out of his ear when it's over. "Thanks for giving my stuff a chance, even if you were totally against following a 'trend.'"

"Thanks for telling me to quit being stubborn and actually *give* it a chance."

"I didn't really make you, but you're welcome."

The song ends and I hand his MP3 player back to him. "I like your guitars and bass the most. You're very talented. I'll listen to the lyrics one of these days. Usually songs go in one ear and out the other unless I really listen. I have to concentrate on both the lyrics and the music for it to make me feel something. Know what I mean? I'm probably not making sense, am I?"

"You're making total sense. And if it makes you feel any better, my stuff didn't always sound like this. It used to be mellow. There are a few mellow songs on the CD, of course, but if you have a little time to kill in New York, I'll take you to my place and play something softer for you."

I stiffen at that. I've never really been back to a guy's "place" before. And I'm supposed to be hunting down my birth mom, not frolicking around a huge city with someone I barely met. "I don't know about that."

He must sense that I'm uncomfortable because he puts a hand on my arm, sending chills through my body. "My family's house." I glance at him and see a soft smile on his face. "Remember?"

"Oh. Right."

"Trust me. I'm not the kind of guy who jumps every girl he meets, contrary to what the tabloids say."

"That's . . . good to know."

"Not that I wouldn't . . ." He trails off and I swear I see a blush tinge his cheeks. Instead of picking up where he left off, he stretches his legs as much as he can and makes himself comfortable. "Anyway. I'll only take you to my *parents'* place if you have a little time to sight-see because Long Island is kind of out of the way. And, I mean, you *have* to see a few things. It's New York. How many chances will you ever get to go there again?"

"Probably none." Since I'll be locked in my room for the rest of my life. "I'll see if I have time. My parents are going to be freaking out as it is."

"Sounds like you guys are pretty close."

"We are. My dad raised me and my sister alone, and then he married a nice lady named Trista when I was ten. She's the only mom I've ever known. They're good for each other." I smile, sadly, thinking of Carmen again. I sometimes wonder how she would have raised us if she hadn't left. Would I be a different person? Would I have been as happy? I can't imagine living my life without Trista. She's been a wonderful mother to me. "They had my brother a few years after they married. His name is Zack. He's a cutie. A redhead like my mom."

"That's cool."

"What about your family? Are you guys close?"

He shrugs. "Depends on what you call close."

"Do you talk on the phone a lot?"

"I talk to my mom at least once a week. My sister Jeigh, usually every day. We've always been really close. I have another sister, but she's a bit younger, so I don't hear from her as much. I love hanging out with her when I go home, though."

"So, you have three in your family and I have three in mine. Another thing we have in common."

"Yes. Yes it is."

I drum my fingers on my knee and wait for him to keep going, but he doesn't, so I change the subject. "So, how far away from the airport is . . . everything? Like downtown New York. That kind of stuff."

The corner of his mouth hints at a smile. "Do you even have any idea where you're going?"

"No clue. I know what the Statue of Liberty looks like. Does that count?"

He snorts and plays with his eyebrow ring. "Not really."

"I know. I should have planned ahead."

"Do you know where your mom lives?"

"I know she's right in New York City, but that's it. And there are two people with the same name. I guess I'll have to try both." I sink down in my seat.

"What hotel are you staying at?"

"Uh . . . A New York one?"

He stares at me a moment, then shakes his head. "You don't have a place to stay, do you?"

"Not exactly. I'll just wing it when I get there."

"I can help."

"No, I don't need help. Thank you, though."

"Where will you sleep?"

"I could sleep in the airport. Do they let people do that? I remember watching a show about a guy living in an airport for a while, but I don't know if it's actually allowed. You know the movies. They make things seem like they're totally fine and normal. But when someone tries it in real life, everything goes to crap."

He shakes his head, a tiny smile on his lips. "I never thought about it that way."

I shrug. "I think about weird things a lot. The weirder, the better. It drives my family crazy. And then sometimes, most of the time I guess, those weird thoughts work their way out into the world, you know?" I'm rambling now. Knowing he knows I don't have a place to stay is making me sweat. I don't like feeling so out of my element, but I am, and from the look he's giving me, he totally knows it. I should have thought things through. Booked something online.

Dumb.

"Eh, I think about weird stuff, too. It's okay." He sits up straighter. "After what you've told me, you sure thought this trip out pretty well, huh?"

I put a hand over my face. "No. I did not. Obviously."

He sits there a moment and leans closer, so our shoulders touch. "You can stay with my family if you'd like."

The thought makes my worries melt away, but then I ask myself if I can trust him. I've only known him about half a day—and even though I know a bit about his family, it's not enough. The offer is sweet, but . . . I should be cautious, shouldn't I? Being spontaneous is one thing, but being stupid is another.

"I don't know, Jaxton. I don't really know you at all. Besides the whole music thing . . . And how you're going through a kind of crisis. But other than that . . ."

"It's Jax."

I glance over at him, his blue eyes soft as he watches me. "You go by Jax?"

"Only to friends and family."

I tuck my hair behind my ear and look away briefly. "Oh. Thanks." I've heard some fans call him that, but the media always use Jaxton.

"So, you won't stay with me because you don't know me. But you also have nowhere else to stay and don't know your way around the city. So . . . let's get to know me a little better, shall we? Some things about me. Hmmm . . ."

"You really don't have to—" I stop midsentence when his face brightens.

"I don't like fast food very much. I'll eat it when I have to. You know, like when we're in an airport and need lunch, but other than that, it's the last thing I'd pick. And it's not because it's fatty or anything, I just like other stuff. Mostly homemade stuff. My mom is an excellent cook. I guess I was spoiled as a child with good cooking."

"Makes sense. I have to be honest, though. I love a juicy fast-food hamburger."

He laughs. "I noticed. And they're okay sometimes." He sits there a second. "Oh. Also . . . I play the bagpipes."

My mouth drops open. "Are you kidding?"

"Nope. My mom was kind of obsessed with our Scottish heritage and made me take lessons as a child. I had to wear a kilt and everything at recitals." He grins. "You better believe I still look good in one."

"Oh dear." I don't doubt that. I'm sure he'd look good in anything.

"I'm actually pretty good."

I bust up laughing. I can't imagine him wearing a kilt and playing the bagpipes at all. That would be a show, I guarantee you. "That's awesome. I'd love to hear you play sometime."

"Do you play anything besides piano?"

"I can play a mean harmonica."

"Really?"

"I really can. Weird, but true. Oh, and I absolutely love thunderstorms. Especially when there is a lot of lightning. And rain. It relaxes me and gets me in the mood to write piano music. I seem to write my best ones when it rains."

"Me, too."

"Really?"

"Yeah. Rain kind of brings a melancholy mood with it. Which usually brings out the best inspiration and lyrical words from inside." He glances at me. "I know. Weird."

"No, I totally get it. Anything else about you?"

"I never sleep past six-thirty in the morning, I go to bed early like I'm sixty."

I laugh at that. "Yeah, I'm a night owl."

"I have to be when I'm on tour, but I love getting a good night's rest every other night. I can't focus well when I'm tired."

"Makes sense."

"I'm a big believer in Karma and all that."

"Me too. I always try to be nice to people, even when I'm annoyed. You never know when you might meet said person again. Maddy is totally nicer than me by far, but I do try."

"You don't seem like you could offend a fly."

"Uh, I offended you."

He laughs. "Not on purpose, though."

"Yeah, I honestly about died when I realized it was you. How embarrassing."

"It will be a great story someday."

"I know," I grumble, which makes him laugh harder.

"Oh, man. So funny. Anyway, what else can I tell you." He screws his face up in concentration, "Oh! I'm slightly deaf in one ear, but no one really knows."

"Which ear?"

He touches his left one. "I can still hear you, just not real well. It doesn't really affect my music, though if it gets worse I may be wearing a hearing aid in a few years. My audiologist has a few tricks up his sleeve for me that I can try when the time comes."

Now I feel bad about getting mad at how loud his MP3 player was. Yet another way to offend him. I'm on a roll today. "Has it always been that way?"

"Yep. Ever since I was a kid. My parents thought I just didn't listen, but when they took me to the doctor for a hearing test, they figured out I really had hearing problems."

"Interesting."

"Also, when I was seven I wanted to be a cowboy when I grew up. Like, I wore cowboy boots, talked with an accent. All of it. I'm glad I grew out of that stage." He laughs.

"Oh, I don't know. Seeing you walk around in cowboy boots and tight pants would probably make your lady fans happy."

"I know," he says, frowning. "Let's see. What else . . . I don't take compliments well, and don't like watching myself sing on TV. It's weird. My favorite color is blue, favorite food is anything Italian, and the one place I've never gone but would love to go is Australia."

"Anything else? Some of those things your fans probably already know through interviews and articles. Tell me something . . . deeper, I guess. Not like, really personal, but something no one would know. Like biggest regret maybe? What you're afraid of?"

He blinks. "What I'm afraid of?"

I shrug. "Everyone's afraid of something."

"What are *you* afraid of?"

"That's easy. My sister dying. It's my worst fear, ever. I can't think about it because it could actually be a reality sooner than later."

"Ugh, I'm so sorry."

"It's just my life right now. As horrible as it is. What about you?"

"I don't really—"

I shake my head. "Never mind. Just ignore me. Sorry. I overstepped. I do that a lot without thinking things through first. I just like seeing people for who they really are. Not just the outside, normal things."

"No problem at all. I've just never been asked that before, so I've never had to think about it." He pauses, his expression curious, like he doesn't really know what to think of me. Then his face turns serious. "My biggest fear, physically, is drowning. I don't know why, but I'm convinced it would be the worst way to die. Seeing the surface so close to your reach and not being able to make it there as the air rushes out of your lungs."

I shudder. "Agreed."

"Mentally, though, is getting to the point where I don't care about anything other than myself."

"I doubt that would ever happen."

"It's a real problem with my lifestyle, though. My buddies are hooked on all kinds of drugs and only live for their next fix. They spend all their hard-earned money on drugs and don't care about anything other than that. They spend their money on things like multiple houses and cars and drop girls like yesterday's trash, just because they can. It's distorted how they think, how they act. I was part of that for a while until I realized it wasn't worth it. I don't ever want to lose myself like that again."

I'm quiet for a moment, taking it all in. He lives such a different life from mine. "I figured that lifestyle is tough from all the overdoses and suicides I read about, but I never dreamed it was so rampant."

"It is. That's one reason I want out."

"I'm sorry."

"Don't be. I chose this life. It's my job to figure out how to change it."

I nod. While I don't understand why anyone would choose that life, and don't relate to it in any way, I do understand how someone could get wrapped up in it when that's all that surrounds you every day. It would be hard to stay true to yourself, when everyone else is falling away.

He's quiet, I assume gathering his thoughts. He looks so serious and I feel bad I made him answer my hard questions. I should think before I talk sometimes.

He stares at one of the magazines stuffed into the chair in front of him and finally speaks again. "My biggest regret, I think, is not finishing my senior year of high school in an actual high school. I missed out on a lot of stuff and I haven't seen some of my friends since my junior year." He taps his knee with his hand. "I was on the track team since my freshman year and loved it. It would be nice to run again. And learn again. I love to learn. Reading is one of my favorite things."

"Me, too. I'm so sorry I brought up painful memories for you, though. Just tell me to shut up next time."

He looks at me, surprised. "Don't be sorry at all. They were really good questions I actually had to think about before I answered. It was refreshing, even. And while we're on the subject, what's your biggest regret?"

"*My* biggest regret?" I frown. "I don't really know . . ." What *is* my biggest regret? I've never really thought about it before. "You're right. This is hard."

He eases into a slow smile. "Hey, you're the one who asked the question."

"I know. I didn't think it would be this hard, though. You've accomplished more than I could ever dream of so far. I haven't really accomplished anything. So,

I guess I regret not setting and reaching more goals to do great things."

"Like what?"

"Oh, I don't know. Pushing myself to get perfect grades. Instead I focused on getting Maddy better and played soccer in my down times. I haven't really cared about my grades. And they're not bad by any means. I could just do better. I know I could."

"Well, this next year, push yourself for a 4.0."

"I think I will. I want to get into a good college. Do you have plans to go to college?"

"I do. I want to study music. Major in it. Maybe teach music to kids. I love kids. They're just so fascinating and smart and funny. I'd love to have a dozen or so of my own."

All I can say is, "Wow."

"I'm joking. I would like a big family, though. Maybe four kids." He chuckles. "Now you've got me talking about my future plans that no one else knows about. Not sure how you managed to get that out of me, too."

I sink lower in my seat and shut my eyes, embarrassed. "Because I'm irresistible to talk to?"

"You're not wrong."

I look up at him. "Sorry. I'm not usually so . . . nosy, I guess."

"You're not being nosy. Just curious. And I like deep conversations, too. I don't have them often."

"Me either."

We're both quiet for a moment. "Well, now you know more about me than 99 percent of my fans. You should feel proud of yourself."

"I am. It was . . . fascinating. Really." I want to turn the conversation light again, so I pull the subject away from hard things. "I still don't believe you play the bagpipes, though."

"That one is definitely true. And they're cool. Maybe I'll put some into one of my future songs."

"That would be awesome. And I think it's so nice that you love kids so much. You're going to make someone very happy someday."

He smiles. "Thanks. But really. Now that you know me a little better, if you need a place to stay, you can stay at my place. My parents won't mind, I promise."

"That doesn't really tell me anything . . . useful, I guess. I mean, useful, yes, but I still don't know what to do."

"I know. It was worth a shot. But I promise to be on my best behavior. And my family is really, well, normal."

"Thank you. I'll think about it."

He bumps my shoulder. "And I'll talk you into it the rest of the flight. We have four more hours, after all."

I chuckle. "Great."

"So, tell me about your sister. Maddy. What's she like?"

I smile. "I'm impressed you remembered her name. I think I only said it once."

He shrugs. "I remember important details. No big deal."

But it is a big deal. This guy is seriously growing on me. Which is stupid. I don't need a crush right now. Especially when I'm doing all this—the flight, New York, hunting down Carmen—for Maddy. If I were on vacation and sight-seeing, a crush and a little romance would be welcome, for sure, but I need to keep my eye on the ball this time. "What do you want to know about her?"

"You two are close, obviously. Do you have the same charming personality?"

That gets a laugh from me and I shake my head. "Ha. No. We're total opposites. The only thing we have in common is our dark hair and skin tone. Maddy is more like our dad. Quiet, reserved, one of the nicest people you'll ever meet. Any good quality you can think of, she probably possesses. Patient, always in a good mood even if there's no reason on earth she should be." I frown. "Then there's me. I'm admittedly loud, impatient, impulsive." I say the last word kind of loud and drawn out, showing him that I don't usually plan things out. He's probably guessed that one already, though; there have been enough hints.

"I have a habit of not thinking things through before I do them," I continue, folding my arms and closing my eyes for a second, feeling a little . . . overwhelmed with what I'm going to have to do when we land. "I don't know if my . . . mom . . . or Carmen, I guess, will even want to see me."

"Why wouldn't she?" It's an honest question, but one I can't really answer.

"I don't think she cares." And that's what is so terrifying about finding her and telling her about Maddy. Knowing she could crush our hope with a single word.

"You don't know that."

I look over at him, surprised at how close our faces are. He looks so concerned, it makes me want to cry. Which I refuse to do in front of a stranger. "For years, my dad has told me she doesn't care about us. And I think I'm starting to believe him. No phone calls, no emails. No cards besides the one I got when I was three right after she left. She left a month before my birthday. Maddy wasn't even a year old yet. You'd think she'd try a little harder to keep in contact with her own daughters if she did care."

"I've figured, you never really know what's going on in someone's life until you've looked inside. Know what I mean?" He leans over and tucks that stupid loose strand of hair behind my ear again. "People think they have a person all figured out, but they're almost never right. Take me, for example. I'm not a perfect person. Far from it. But I'm not a huge screw-up either. The world has painted a picture of me being this party guy who doesn't think about anything but getting drunk or getting high. Whatever the stories are. Because that's what my band does. But if they knew the real me, they'd be surprised how normal I am. Sure I have problems to deal with, but I'm not as crazy as everyone thinks." He smiles. "It's all part of the Hollywood image. Be controversial. Be different. Don't ever be yourself. That's the biggest lie celebrities tell their fans. No one really knows them. Besides a few close people they care about."

"Like family."

He shrugs. "And a few friends." He winks at me and my stomach flips.

"I don't know what it is about you," he says, "but you make me feel . . . safe. I can trust you." He chuckles and shakes his head. "That sounds so stupid, but I don't know another way to describe it."

"It doesn't sound stupid," I assure him. I've been fighting the same feeling, but I don't say that aloud.

"It does a little. I just mean, I feel like I don't have to worry about you spilling all my secrets to the press or anything. Because I don't really want everyone to know about me playing the bagpipes. Or the whole cowboy thing. Or you know. My worst fears. Please keep that under wraps, deal?"

"Deal." And I'm serious.

He leans his head closer to me, if that's possible. "Thanks for letting me vent to you. It's nice to talk to someone so . . . normal." His eyes grow wide. "But normal is not a bad thing, I promise. Far from it."

"Thanks."

He stares at me for a second before blinking once and glancing away. He doesn't sit up, though, or scoot away. And I can't help but notice it's suddenly very stuffy and hard to breathe in here. Who knew you could find out so much about a person just by sitting next to them for a few hours on a plane?

I don't know everything about him, but he feels like he's told me a lot. He probably knows way more about me since I've been talking all day, though. But the glimpses of his life that he's shared with me are so interesting. A boy who's stuck, trying to please the world around him by being someone else. Because part of him is broken. I can tell by the way his hands shake in his lap. The little habit of playing with his eyebrow ring. Like a nervous tick. The way the dark circles stand out under his eyes. I hadn't noticed them until I got so close to him, but they're prominent now. I sense an underlying sadness that he tries to keep bottled up, but when he lets his guard down for even a split second, I see it. He tries so hard to keep it hidden, but he's only human. A person can only hide so much pain and disappointment until it becomes too much to keep in. It eventually finds its way out.

It always does.

And for some strange reason, I really want to help him. To take away whatever demons or shadows are eating at him. Take the pain away. Celebrity or not, he's a person just like me. And we're more alike than I ever thought possible.

The thought of it kind of scares me. I've never had a connection like this before. I'm not sure what I'm supposed to do with it.

We're two people running from different things in our lives. One of us is running to save another, the other is running to save himself.

I'm not sure which journey will be more difficult.

CHAPTER 13

These words inside my head
Aren't for just anyone to see
They belong to you and you alone
The one who set them free
—J.S.

The hours tick by, and Jax and I talk the entire time. I tell him about home. What my junior year of high school was like. Being the pianist for the concert choir and playing soccer on the varsity team. I think of my soccer teammates. They are some of my very favorite people and dearest friends. I tell Jax about the fundraiser they set up for Maddy's medical bills last year. I had no idea they were doing it and it brought me and my family to tears.

He tells me more about playing with his band in high school, getting honors, even though people thought he didn't care about grades, and stupid things he did with his friends.

I feel my body getting tired, since it's almost eleven at night on the west coast, but I don't want to miss any of our conversation. After my third yawn, though, he shakes his head. "You can sleep if you need to. We still have an hour or two before we get there."

"I'm fine, really." I yawn again and he laughs.

"Take a nap. You can even lean on me if you want."

I freeze at that. As much as I want to, I don't want to make either one of us uncomfortable. "I'll just . . . uh . . . lean my head back for a little bit."

He shrugs. "If you insist. Shoulders are more comfortable, though."

"Not if they're bony."

I hear his deep, quiet laugh as I close my eyes.

"If I couldn't have sat by you, I probably would have slept the entire flight," he whispers.

"I wouldn't. The guy next to me would have thrown up in my lap."

"Nasty."

"So, if you would have slept the entire flight if I wouldn't have moved, what are you trying to say? That you're tired and really do need sleep? That I'm a talker who you can't get to shut up?"

I open one eye to gauge his reaction, but his eyes are closed and he's smiling. "Something like that."

I smack him softly in the arm and his eyes pop open.

"Ouch. Maybe I should have the flight attendant come move you to a different seat so I can get some sleep. I probably could get away with something like that if I told her who I am, you know."

"You wouldn't dare," I grumble.

"Wouldn't I?" He winks and closes his eyes again, his arms folded across his chest.

"You're hilarious." I let out a slow, easy breath and close

my eyes, as well. The plane is super quiet and someone snores softly a few rows behind us. As long as the snoring doesn't get out of hand, I'll hopefully be able to drift off. If not, I may have to go plug someone's nose.

♫

I'm not sure how much time has passed, but the next thing I know, I'm opening my eyes. For a moment, I've forgotten where I am, but as I recognize the seats in front of me and feel someone leaning into me—and smell his cologne—I remember.

My head rests on Jax's shoulder and he's using my hair as a pillow. When I realize my hand is on his chest, I don't move, but my body temperature definitely rises a few degrees. My hand rises and falls with the steady rhythm of his breathing and I'm positive he's asleep.

Just wait until Maddy hears about his. She'll *freak*.

I shift my body a little, and Jax yawns and sits up. "Sorry," I say, removing my hand as fast as possible. "Didn't mean to wake you."

"Hey," he says. I can hear the smile in his voice as I sit up straight and smooth my hair down. I'm sure I look fabulous.

I take a few seconds to clear my throat; I don't want to sound all seductive with my tired voice. "Hey." The smile I give him is shy. I can tell, but he doesn't seem to notice.

He yawns. "How long have I been out?"

"No idea. Not very long, I'd guess."

"Good. I don't normally take naps on people who sit by me, but I have to admit, you were pretty comfortable."

I fold my arms and shy away from him. "Thanks, I think." I sneak a glance at him. He's watching me with the corner of his mouth turned up.

We stare at each other for a moment before he clears his throat. "So, you don't have a place to stay tonight, right?"

"No. I should have thought this whole thing out better, I know. I just acted. Spontaneity is supposed to be good for you. Most of the time." *Stop talking, Mia.*

"Well, Mia." He smiles. "Mia. Have I told you I really like that name?"

"Uh . . . no?"

He smiles wider and I look away from his gaze. "Have you decided if you want to stay with me yet?"

I hesitate. "I don't know . . ."

"You know, I can help you find a hotel if that would be better," he says just as fast. "Whatever makes you more comfortable."

My parents would murder me if they found out I slept at some random guy's house. I guess Jax isn't really random in that way, a random rockstar, but I know they'd still freak. "I think a hotel would be better."

"It's settled then. There's a place I stay that overlooks Central Park. I'll call it in as soon as we land."

"Oh, no. No way. There's no way I can afford something like that." I've heard of the apartments and hotels overlooking Central Park. I know the park is freaking huge, but I know the prices are super high.

"No worries, Mia. I can." He winks, and the way he looks at me signals the end of the conversation.

CHAPTER 14

Lyrics are the stories of the cheated, broken, and misunderstood. Through music is the only way their voices will ever be heard.
—J.S.

The descent into New York makes my ears go crazy. Jax hands me a piece of gum to hopefully pop my ears before they blow up, but even with my overenthusiastic chewing, they still hurt. As the plane touches down, I realize my stomach is in knots. And I sort of feel like I'm going to throw up. Which would be a complete disaster. With my luck, the paparazzi would recognize Jax and plaster a picture of me puking on Jax's shoe for the whole world to see.

It hasn't even happened and I'm kind of freaking out about it. Because it could. I'm a recipe for disaster, or whatever that stupid cliché is.

"You ready for this?" Jax stands as I pull my bag down from the overhead. I glance up at him. Even after that nap, he still looks exhausted. I wonder how long it's been since he slept well.

"Not really." And it's true. I don't know what to think right now. What I'll say to Carmen when I see her. If I see her. No. *When* I see her. Because I'm going to find her no matter what.

But what will I do when I do see her? Will I feel anything? Will I cry? Laugh? Cry tears of joy when I finally embrace my birth mother for the first time in years? Or will I focus on my temper and yell at her for abandoning me? What would Maddy do?

She'd stay calm, of course. But the emotional possibilities of what *I* will do are endless and, frankly, I'm kind of terrified of what I might feel. I have no idea which emotion will grace itself at the right time. I was a child when she left, so I didn't have room for much emotion then. But if I've been bottling it up for the last fifteen years, there may be a problem when it all comes pouring out.

I'm afraid of what she'll see. What I'll do.

I'm quiet as we follow the other passengers down the jetway and through our gate. Jax grabs my elbow, gently, and leads me through the terminal. In the direction of . . . I'm not sure. This place is really big and kind of intimidating. Lots of professional-looking people in suits holding briefcases or talking on cells.

I notice a lady sitting on a big suitcase in a waiting area by the baggage claim. She looks like every executive businesswoman I've seen in the movies. Her hair's in a tight bun, her makeup perfect, and her dress is . . . er . . . short? So short I wouldn't be sitting like *that* in it. Actually, I probably couldn't sit in it at all. But she looks totally relaxed with her super long legs crossed and her five-inch high heels on her feet, lazily scrolling through her phone. A few smaller suitcases sit next to her and suddenly I'm super happy with my packing choices. I don't have to hunt down any luggage. Or worry about it getting lost. Which is awesome. And weird for me. My wardrobe back home isn't exactly small.

"You okay?" Jax asks as we weave through the crowd.

Somehow, I'd forgotten he was with me for a minute. "Yeah." Once this whole trip is over, hopefully the world will right itself. No more running off to places I've never been before, no more talking to strange guys on airplanes, no more wondering if Maddy is going to make it another year. Everything will be normal again. It has to be.

We pass a few people standing in the lobby holding signs with random names on them. There are a few taxi drivers, some really well dressed people (movie star agents or something?), and a group of tourists wearing the same red shirts and hugging each other. And when I say group, I mean like twenty of them. They all seem so happy to see one another, and I assume they're family, flying from different parts of the country and meeting in New York to explore together. You can see the love they have for each other radiating off them. It makes me miss my family. I shake my head. I haven't even been gone twelve hours and I'm already homesick? What the heck is wrong with me?

Before I get lost in the crowd, Jax grabs my hand and pulls me along with him. And not just a *hey there, hang on to me so you don't get lost* kind of hand hold. More like a *back off, this girl is mine* kind of hand hold. If there is such a hold. Also, I'm sure I'm overanalyzing everything. But what else am I supposed to do at the moment? Besides. I'm a girl. It's what we do best. Overanalyzing for the win!

My free hand tightens on my bag and luckily my purse is wrapped around my shoulder. With nothing else to worry about, we walk through the crowded airport together and one thought keeps running through my mind ahead of the others:

I'm holding Jaxton Scott's hand. I'm holding Jaxton Scott's hand. I'm freaking holding Jaxton Scott's freaking hand.

Relax, Mia. He's a person. All people have hands. Quit making this a big deal when it's not.

It totally is.

I swear, I don't have multiple personalities.

Actually . . . maybe I do.

Shut up, Mia.

We walk through the glass doors that lead outside. I've forgotten how late it is and am surprised to find the sky so dark.

"Are we getting a taxi?" I stare at all the taxis sitting next to the curb, wondering if Jax typically rides in them or if he has his own limo service, when he raises his free hand and waves at someone.

"Nope. I've got our ride covered."

He pulls me past a bunch of taxis and grins at a girl about our age in a cute red tank and shorts who's standing next to a super nice car. She's talking on her cell, oblivious to us at the moment, but when she looks up and sees us,

119

she hangs up on whoever she was talking to and squeals really—really—loud.

"Jax!"

I shouldn't be surprised to see a girl picking him up. He is a rockstar, after all. But even so, a little prick of jealousy creeps under my skin. Which is stupid. It's not like we're dating or anything. I'm just a girl from California who hasn't had a boyfriend since her sophomore year of high school.

And she doesn't talk about that boyfriend.

Because Kevin was an idiot. And so was I for going out with him.

Jax lets go of my hand and rushes to the girl, picking her up and spinning her around. The girl laughs and wraps her arms around his neck, hugging him super tight, which makes me look away. This whole thing just got super awkward and I'm second-guessing my spur of the moment decision to take him up on his offer to find me a hotel room.

"I'm so happy you're here, Jax!" the girl says. "When Mom said you were coming for the weekend, I was so excited. I didn't think you'd be back so soon. With your tours and everything, I thought it would be another three months at least."

My ears perk up at the word *mom*. She's his sister. Jeigh, I believe, from what he said on the plane. He said they were close. My body relaxes and I release a long breath.

"I needed a little break, so I'm here for a few days. I wish it were longer."

"We'll take what we can get."

I study them. You can tell just by looking at them that they are definitely close. Why I was being weird about this is beyond me. Like we're even a couple. Like we're even really friends. We've known each other for what? Seven hours?

I really need to get a life. And possibly a date.

Someday.

I have to save my sister first.

Jax reaches out a hand and pulls me over to them and then drapes an arm around my shoulder. "Mia, this is Jeigh. My little sister. Jeigh, this is Mia."

She rolls her eyes. "Do you really have to say little sister when you introduce me to someone? Come on. We're like, a year apart."

"It's true, isn't it?"

Jeigh is gorgeous. Black hair against her white skin. Dainty and short. She kind of has a Snow White vibe going on, but no red lips here. She reaches out her hand and I take it, giving it a good shake. I hate wimpy handshakes so I always try to squeeze hard. Sometimes I get some weird looks, but other times, like this time, the hand-shaker appreciates a good grip.

"It's nice to meet you, Jeigh." I love how out of all the people in Jax's life, his sister is the one who picks him up from the airport. No limo driver, no agent. His sister. I think about Maddy. I know she'd be the one I'd want by my side if I were in Jax's situation. And she totally would be there for me, too.

"It's nice to meet you, too, Mia." Her smile is genuine and so white and pretty it makes me want to go bleach my teeth. She glances at Jax, a grin on her face. "Mom didn't say you were bringing a girl with you."

He pulls his baseball cap down and his cheeks turn pink. "I'm not. I mean, she's not coming home with us. She's going to stay by Central Park tonight. Then I'll take her to see the city tomorrow."

"Ah. I get it." She looks at me, her eyes widening. "First time in New York?"

"Yep."

"Awesome. If you get tired of Jax, I'll be happy to show you around. I'm the fun one in the family. Jax is all business most of the time. Boring." She nudges me in the shoulder and I laugh. I like her already.

"Whatever." Jax punches her softly in the arm and looks over at me. "You ready?"

I shrug. "Whenever you are. I have no idea where I'm going."

"Let's get to it then." He grabs my bag from me, opens the back door of the car, and sets it on the seat. I move to sit in the back with it, but he opens the passenger door and gestures inside. "You get shotgun."

"But—"

"I insist." He grins and gets in the back, leaving me no choice but to sit in the front.

Seriously. Whoever said chivalry was dead hasn't met this guy. He could teach the guys at home a thing or two.

Jeigh gets in the driver's seat and we're off.

And I swear my life flashes before my eyes a dozen times before we make it into the city.

She's a crazy driver. But every time Jax yells something at her, or swears under his breath, she assures us everything's fine. "I'm used to driving around here. No worries." She slams on the brakes again and my stomach lurches as we stop two inches from the car in front of us.

"Jeigh? Has Mom ridden with you lately?" Jax asks. I glance in the backseat. He looks a little pale. "You drive like a cabby."

"I'll take that as a compliment, seeing how we're in New York. You have to be a little crazy to navigate these roads. As for Mom riding with me, that would be a negative. I usually go it alone. Or I take Justice with me."

"Please don't put her life in danger. She's the baby."

"Baby?" I ask.

Jeigh glances at me. "She's fifteen. And the youngest in the fam. Jax is the oldest." Justice, Jeigh, and Jax. Their parents must really like J's.

"Cool. I'm the oldest too. Um . . . keep your eyes on the road? Please?" I whimper as she finally looks at the road and slams on the brakes again. My hands hit the dash and I breathe in and out through my nose.

It's cool. She's cool. Everything's fine.

"You okay up there?" Jax asks.

"I'm good," I squeak.

Jeigh laughs. "I told you guys. We're fine. I'm in total control. No reason to worry your cute little heads about, you know, your lives or anything."

Jax bursts out laughing behind us. "Yeah, I'd never worry about that while *you're* driving me around."

She grins in the rearview at him. "Like I said. Total control."

I sit back in my seat, debating closing my eyes for the remainder of the ride. But I'm pretty sure I'd be throwing up on the floor if I did that. So I stare straight ahead, digging my fingernails into the leather seat and praying we don't rear-end someone every time she stops the car.

Stop and go traffic is bad in Cali, but it's nothing compared to here.

There's no way I'd ever drive here. Ever.

Taxis are everywhere. So many cars fight to change lanes. I get it now—why people walk or ride the subway everywhere instead of drive. The roads are straight out of a nightmare.

When I've calmed down a bit and gotten used to Jeigh's driving (kind of), we get into the big parts of the city. I marvel at how huge the buildings are and at all the lighted windows that rise high in the sky. The movies don't do them justice. The buildings are seriously huge. And honestly, staring up at them kind of makes me a little claustrophobic.

"Central Park is on your right," Jax says.

I glance out the window, my eyes wide, taking everything in. It's dark, so I can't see the awesomeness of it all, but it's there. And it's amazing.

Jeigh takes a left and zooms up next to the curb. Or . . . on the curb. "Well, here's your stop."

Jax gets out first and I follow. He hands me my bag and leans back in the car. "I'll be back in a sec." He glances around outside. "Lock the doors."

Jeigh rolls her eyes. "I'll be fine. I keep a bat in here to scare people off." She reaches around her seat and holds up a baseball bat, a grin sliding into place.

Jax stares at her. "Seriously? A bat?"

"Hey, I won our high school championship last year with this baby. I know how to swing it if I need to."

He shakes his head.

"It was nice to meet you, Mia!" she says, dropping the bat in the back seat.

"You too!"

Jax shuts the door and stands next to the car until Jeigh locks the doors. I rub my bare arms at the slight breeze and follow him through the double glass doors and into the hotel.

And what a hotel it is. It's huge. Clean. Freaking amazing. There's no way he's letting me stay here at his expense. But before I can stop him, Jax takes off his hat and calmly walks up to the registration desk. The woman behind the desk taps her red nails on the counter as she talks to one of the bellhops. (I think that's what they're called.)

"Hello, Caroline. Can I get one of my usual rooms please?"

The woman jumps and her face spreads into a grin. "Mr. Scott! How nice to see you. You'd like a room for tonight?"

"Yes, please."

"Of course, sir." She types something into the computer sitting on the desk. "We have a suite all ready for you." She turns around and grabs a card, hands it to him, and glances over the desk. "No luggage?"

"Not today. My friend will be staying here, so please get her anything she needs and put it on my tab."

"Of course, sir." She smiles, gives me the once over, and waves as we start toward the elevator.

I'm feeling super small right now. And inconvenient. And . . . I don't know. Poor. I don't want him to think I'm incapable of paying for things, but I also don't want him to know I don't come from a wealthy family and I've never even been inside a hotel this nice.

I mean, we were always comfortable and had enough. But right now I feel like an ant getting squished under a rich person's shoe. "You didn't have to pay for this," I mutter as I try to think of ways to make myself look more presentable.

He shrugs. "I know. But I want to."

"You don't have to. I can find somewhere else to stay. Really. I feel awful. I swear I'm not a leech or one of those girls who just wants to get in your pants or something for a one night stand. I'm not using you for your money."

He laughs. "Trust me. I'd know by now if you were one of those girls."

That makes me feel a little better. In a weird way. "Oh. Good. But I really don't want to inconvenience you. I don't ask for favors. I never ask for money. And here you are, paying for my room for the night and I honestly don't

126

know if I can handle this kind of pressure. There's no way to make it up to you. What do you give a person who has everything?"

"Mia." His voice is calm, quiet, and makes my breath catch at the seriousness of the sound. I stop my nervous rambling and look up at him.

He leans toward me. "I want to help you out. I'm the one who offered you the room, so you owe me nothing. I promise you're okay. So please stop freaking out. Honestly, you're kind of freaking *me* out."

"Oh." He's smiling, so I know he's joking about being freaked out. Maybe. "Sorry. About all that. I just get . . . chatty when I'm nervous. And weird."

"I've noticed." The tension rolls off my shoulders a bit as we step into the elevator. He scans the card the lady in the lobby gave him, types in a password, and the elevator rises.

And rises.

Almost up to the very top. The elevator door opens and we walk down a narrow hall. I see only two doors, and I follow him to the one at the end of the hall and on my right. I hear loud music coming from the one on the left.

There's another key reader by the door. "Wow. This is high tech. Hotels usually have key readers, but we usually don't have to put a password in."

"It's more of a hassle than anything." He types in a password, then slides his card in the key reader. The green light blinks, the door opens, and my jaw drops. This place is amazing. White carpets, red couches, huge windows overlooking the city. A small kitchen with a fridge, oven, and microwave. And that's only the stuff in this one room.

Jax walks around, checking out everything. "The bedroom is over here." He walks to the right and I follow. He goes through the bedroom door, flips the light on, and my eyes bug out of my head. I swear the bedroom is bigger than my whole house back home.

The four-poster-bed has a million red and cream pillows on it, and I can't even imagine what the sheets feel like. Silky? What's a good thread count? Like 600? 2000? I have no idea. But I'm sure they're nice. And I'll bet some of those pillows are super comfy, too.

I'm really tired.

Jax glances under the bed, which makes me smile. He seems to be looking for something because he checks the closet and the bathroom, too. When he's finally satisfied, he folds his arms and leans against the bedroom doorframe. He looks exhausted.

"Everything's good. I even checked for monsters." He grins, but it doesn't quite meet his eyes.

"Monsters? Really?" I fold my arms and narrow my eyes.

"You never know."

I chuckle. But for real. I'm secretly glad he did that so I don't have to do it later.

He yawns and covers his mouth until he's done. "You okay then?"

"Jax, I can't even . . . I have no words. Thank you." Without thinking, I reach out and hug him. Not a huge hug, but enough for him to hug me back. His hands slide up my back and I can't help but breathe him in.

"You're welcome." We stand that way for a moment too long and I feel his heart beating wildly against his chest. Our arms both lower at the same time and I take an awkward step back, tucking my hair behind my ear, my own heart doing its own crazy dance.

"Sorry," I start. "I don't—that was . . . Weird. I don't randomly hug people. At least not until the first date."

He stares at me a second and chuckles as he reaches up to play with his eyebrow ring. "Well, how about I take you out tomorrow."

"I kind of have other plans. You know. Finding my birth mom and stealing a kidney from her."

He doesn't even flinch. "That's not disturbing at all."

"Nope." I chuckle and rub a hand over my tired eyes. "You know what I mean. I can't think this late. Coherently, at least."

"You need to get some sleep. We both do, I think. So, how about this: tomorrow you can track down your birth mom and I'll keep you hydrated and fed all day. Sound okay?"

"Sounds perfect." I don't even hesitate, realizing there's no one I'd rather spend the day with than him. A not quite complete stranger. Who looks tired and beautiful and sweet all at the same time.

He claps his hands together. "Great. It's a date. If you need anything, call this number." He whips out his pen, grabs a notepad from the bedside table, and scribbles it down. "Can you text me so I can have yours?"

"Are you really asking for my phone number?"

"Maybe." His gaze knocks the wind out of me and I take a step back.

I'm tongue tied for a moment, trying to figure out how the heck I got myself into this wonderful and confusing situation. "I'll text you as soon as I call my parents."

"I'll hold you to it." He heads toward the door. "There are towels, toiletries, whatever you need in the bathroom. If you need something specific, let downstairs know. They'll bring it up."

"Okay." Like I'd ever call downstairs for anything. I can deal with whatever they have in the room already. I'm not picky.

"Well," he rocks on his feet, his eyes never leaving my face. "Today was fun. You made my flight ten times more bearable than if I'd been by someone else."

"You too."

He blinks once. Twice. A shy smile later, he clears his throat and backs out of the bedroom and into the living area. I follow him until he reaches the door. "I'll see you tomorrow then."

"Okay. Thank you. Again. For letting me stay here."

"It's my pleasure." He looks like he wants to say something else, but he just shakes his head. And with that, he walks out the door and leaves me alone.

I look around the huge living space and suddenly feel so . . . lonely. I kind of wish he'd stayed here with me. Not . . . With me-with me. But in the same place. Room. Apartment. Whatever.

Not that it wouldn't be totally weird and everything, since we just met, but he seems to have this calming effect on me.

Speaking of calm . . . I haven't checked my messages since we landed. I'm sure my parents are anything but calm. I pull out my phone, turn it on, and find three voicemails and eleven text messages.

Cringing, I push the voicemails first, prepared for angry voices.

It's Dad. Lots of swearing, lots of yelling, threats to ground me forever, take away my car, lock me in my room for the rest of my life. Everything he's probably always wanted to say to me at one time or another. I get them all at the same time.

Angry is an understatement. Hopefully he's cooled down enough to talk now, since the last voicemail was an hour ago. Instead of reading all the angry texts, I call him back.

He picks up on the first ring. "Mia." His voice is anything but calm. It's low. Furious.

"Hey, Dad," I say, testing the waters a little.

"Are you out of your mind? What has gotten into you? What in the world went through your head that made you just randomly jump on a plane and fly to New York? New York, Mia. Really? You've never been anywhere near there. You have no idea where you're going or what you're going to find. Where are you? Are you still in the airport? I'll give you my credit card number right now and fly you home tonight."

"Dad, calm down. I just got here. I've been on an airplane all day, so I'm not coming home tonight."

"You are."

"No. I'm not. I'm eighteen years old. I can do things like this now. I don't need you with me and I don't need your permission."

"Mia . . ."

"Just listen to me. Please. I'm at a hotel. I'll text you the details. I'm totally fine." At the moment, I guess.

"You're not fine. You're in New York by yourself. There is nothing about this whole situation that's *fine*." He says something to someone in the background, but I can't understand what it is.

"Dad." I say it as calm as possible and I hear him take a deep breath, so I take my chance. "How's Maddy?"

"She's . . . fine."

"Good. Does she know where I went?"

A pause. "Yes."

"She didn't know, I swear, so don't get mad at her. I left a note for you and Mom and that's it. I left before I told her where I was going."

"I know. I read your happy little note. Your mother is worried sick about you. And so am I. If anything happens to you . . ." He chokes on the last word.

"I'm fine, Dad. Really. I'm at a hotel and tomorrow I'm going to find Carmen." Another pause. "Dad?"

He sniffs. "Honey, I just want to tell you, she's . . . not like you. Or me."

"I kind of figured that, but Dad, I have to try. I know

you say she won't do anything, and maybe she won't. But if she at least knows about Maddy—if I can tell her how serious it is, how little time she has left—maybe she'll help us."

I wait for him to argue, but he doesn't. "You know I trust you. And I'm sorry you felt like you had to sneak behind my back to do this." He laughs, but it's not his real laugh. It's more . . . nervous than anything. "I don't know why I didn't think you wouldn't do something like this. I've raised you for eighteen years. You'd think I'd be prepared by now."

I smile as I pick flakes of nail polish off my nails. "Yeah, you know me."

He clears his throat and sniffs. "You have her address?"

I hesitate. "Uh . . . not exactly. There were two Carmens listed on the Internet, which isn't bad, but I'll probably have to go to both houses to find the right one. I'm sure I can recognize her from your old pictures. Or picture, I guess."

He pauses again, and when he speaks, it's quieter than before. "She's in Greenpoint." He sighs as though he's just told his deepest, darkest secret and I wish I were next to him so I could give him the biggest hug ever. "That's where her family lives, and I'm assuming she's still around there. If not, they'll help you. They were always very kind. Her mother and sister, especially." I know he's been protecting me all these years, and I'm sure it took a lot for him to give me that tiny piece of information. An address. One simple address that could change our future for the better, or unravel all of my plans. Either way, I'm ready to do this. For Maddy.

Emotion fills my senses and I don't realize my eyes are watering until the room gets blurry. "Thanks, Dad. And I'm sorry I sort of ran away. Not really, but you know what I mean."

He's quiet for a moment, his light breathing all I can hear on the other end. "Please. Be careful, Mia. You have no idea what's out in that city."

"I'll be fine, Dad. I won't go out at night. I won't talk to strangers. I won't go down any creepy alleys or go to a bar with my fake ID."

No laughter or chuckles. I shouldn't have joked.

"You're not making me feel any better, Mia."

"Sorry. I was trying to lighten the mood a little."

"I noticed. But the moment wasn't the right one." He's not amused. "New York is a big place. I want you to go straight to Carmen's tomorrow, do whatever it is you have to do, and catch the first plane possible to come home. Promise me."

"I will." I debate on telling him about Jax, but decide against it. If he knows I'm hanging out with a rocker and staying in his hotel room, he'll find a way to jump through the phone and beat the crap out of him. It's better to leave it alone until later. I'll explain everything then. "I'll let you know when I get a flight. Okay?"

He breathes a sigh of relief. "Okay. Now, make sure your door is locked, don't let anyone in your room, and get some sleep."

"I will."

We're both quiet, neither one of us says good-bye first.

"Thank you, Daddy. For trusting me enough to let me do this."

"You know I wouldn't have let you go, but I have to remember you're not my baby girl anymore. So as angry as I was and still am that you did this without telling me or your mother, I know it's because you care about your sister so much. And speaking of Maddy, she's right here and wants to talk to you."

"Okay." The phone makes a rustling sound and I hear Dad in the background now. "Maddy?"

"I knew you were planning something crazy, but not this crazy." She sounds brighter than earlier but still tired.

"You know me. I'm sorry I didn't tell you."

"It's fine."

"How are you feeling?"

She hesitates, and when she speaks I can hear the frown in her voice. "I'm okay. Just bored and ready to go home."

"Have they said when you'll be able to?"

"No."

"Let me know if you get any worse, okay?"

"I'm fine. A souvenir would cheer me up, though. And make it a cool one."

I laugh. "If I can scrounge up enough pennies, I will."

"I knew you loved me."

"You know I do. I'll talk to you soon, okay?"

"Okay."

"Tell Mom and Dad I love them. And Zack, too."

"Will do. Goodnight."

"Night."

I end the call and let out a long sigh that seems to echo through the huge bedroom. The huge, *creepy* bedroom. I'm not used to so much space. I'm really glad Jax checked for monsters now.

And that reminds me . . . I grab the piece of paper with Jax's number on it and type it into my phone. He told me to text him, so after a moment of internal freak-out, I do.

Me: Here's my number. Thanks for everything.

The phone blinks two seconds later.

Jax: Yes. It worked. I got your number.
Me: Haha. You're tricky.
Jax: I try. Get some rest. See you tomorrow.
Me: ☺

I smile and send Dad a quick text so he knows where I'm staying and shove the phone back in my pocket, wondering how I ended up texting a rockstar.

After getting ready for bed, I grab some blankets off the bed and drag them into the other room and onto the couch. Might as well make it a real sleepover. It's brighter in the living area with the New York lights shining all around and it feels more . . . comfortable.

I lay there for a while, the whole day feeling like a blur. I still can't believe I'm here, by myself, ready to hunt down Carmen to beg her to save Maddy's life. I know what I have to do. The problem is, I'm terrified to do it.

Having Jax with me makes me feel a little braver. And at least he knows how to get around the city.

With a few tosses and turns, and one more glance toward the glow of lights out the window, I drift off to sleep.

CHAPTER 15

Through all the bad times and the good
I'll always be misunderstood.
They look and chase and try to follow
Never leave me. Hard to swallow
They try to find truth when they look in my eyes
But all I can give are secrets and lies
Secrets and lies are a part of me
A part I hope you cannot see.
—J.S.

Someone's knocking on the door. My eyes fly open and bright sunlight is shooting me in the face. I close my eyes, seeing light dots, and pull the covers over my head, remembering Dad's words last night.

Don't open the door for anyone.

Who would be knocking this early? I guess it's not too early, since the sun's up, but early for me.

Tap, tap, tap. "Room service," a high voice says.

Pretty sure I can make an exception for that. I'm starving. I kick my blankets off and shuffle over to the door. One look out the peephole confirms the woman's voice is that of a hotel employee. She's holding a tray of silver platters with silver lids.

I get free breakfast at this hotel? Sweet.

My stomach growls. I don't really want anyone to see me just yet, so I clear my throat. "Just leave it there. I'll get it in a moment. Thank you so much."

The woman nods and sets the tray on the floor before walking down the hall and into the elevator.

I open the door, take a quick glance around, and grab the tray like I'm some kind of starving animal. Once I have the door locked again, I take the tray to the couch. Whatever is underneath the three silver platters smells delicious. I take the biggest one's lid off and grin. French toast. With whipped cream and strawberries. Holy freak, I'm in Heaven.

My phone dings and I glance at the text message. It's from Jax, and I can't stop the smile from creeping to my face.

Jax: Thought you could use a little pick-me-up. I've always been a fan of French Toast. Hopefully it's to your liking. I'll be there in an hour to show you around the city. –J

I type a quick reply, refraining from using "heck yes" or "I'm dying to see you" or "take me I'm yours." A simple "sounds good and thank you" works great. And isn't stalker-ish. But for real—how nice can the guy get?

After wolfing down the French toast, hashbrowns, and eggs, I jump in the shower, get dressed, and have my hair done in record time. Ponytails are the best.

I stare at my reflection for a second and take a deep breath. I'm going to meet my birth mom today. My stomach drops and I make a face at myself. I wonder if I look like her. Would I recognize her on the street? Will she remember me? Will she save Maddy?

How different would my life be if I'd have grown up in New York with her?

I let my thoughts stew while I wait for Jax. What I say and how I act could be the difference between Maddy living or dying. I have to make my visit count.

I wish Mom and Dad were with me.

Someone knocks on the door an hour later and I peek out, smiling as I hurry and open the door.

"Hey," Jax says, his hands in his pockets.

"Hey." I surprise myself by not stuttering.

"Did you enjoy your breakfast?"

"I did. Thank you."

He looks amazing. He's wearing a red shirt, jeans, and a baseball cap with SF on the front. Must love the Giants. I keep the fact that I'm a Dodgers fan to myself and note that he smells amazing. Too much cologne always makes me gag, but I must really like him, because I'm pretty sure he could be wearing a whole gallon of it and I'd still be cool with it.

He grins and backs up a step. "So . . . You ready?"

I'm staring at him like a fool. "Oh. Yes! Let me just grab my purse." I rush inside, grab my phone, and shove it in my purse. I do a once-over in the mirror, even though I know exactly what I looked like two minutes ago, and shut the door behind me.

We walk down the hall and I'm still trying to get my purse situated. It's so messy. Which makes me think: how does a purse manage to get so messy? All I should have in it are keys and my wallet. But no. Random pieces of makeup, a bunch of receipts from fast food runs, a handful of loose change, tickets from a concert I went to like six months ago, a brush, the card Carmen sent me, and . . . A random sock?

Really. I've got to do a major clean out when I get back.

"So, do you want to see your mom first? Er, birth mom?" Jax asks.

I wince. "Uh . . . maybe?" Not really, but yes.

An easy smile as he pushes the elevator button. "Are you nervous?"

Yes. Terrified. "I'm good."

"Great. Why don't you give me the address and we'll track her down then."

"Okay." I dig through my purse again and pull out the paper I wrote the address on, which Dad texted to me late last night because he knew I'd forget. Of course.

"Greenpoint. That's a nicer area. You lucked out." He waits for me to step onto the elevator and follows me inside.

The sound of crappy elevator music fills my ears instead of the silence between us. You know how awkward elevator rides are with people you don't know? That's kind of how I feel right now. We both just stand there and look anywhere but at each other. I don't know where the awkwardness came from, but I can feel it all around and can't handle it anymore.

"You . . . uh . . . know where Greenpoint is then?"

"Of course." The elevator opens, thank the heavens, and we walk into the lobby.

"Have a nice day, Mr. Scott," the hotel manager says.

He nods at her. "You, too. Thanks for everything."

I hurry to catch up to him. "You stay here often?"

He shrugs. "When I have to."

I'm guessing it's a lot.

Jax calls a cab and, before I know it, we're headed toward Greenpoint.

I've never ridden in a cab before. It kind of smells like grease and cigarettes mixed with old pizza and beer, which sounds about right for a cab. Another smell assaults my nose as I switch positions in the seat.

Stinky feet.

Nice.

"First time in a cab?" Jax asks, a smirk on his face.

"That obvious?"

He chuckles. "Nah, you look like you've done this a million times." He gives me a goofy grin and I punch him in the shoulder.

My eyes fall to his tattoo and, before I can stop myself, I touch it. "How long have you had this?"

"About a year."

I trace the lines with my finger and pull away when I notice him shiver. "Sorry."

"Don't be sorry." The corner of his mouth turns up and he looks away. "I got it last year after my dad died."

My heart feels like it stops for a second, and I feel so bad that I have no words. "I had no idea. I'm so sorry."

"You didn't see the headlines?"

I shake my head. "I told you I don't keep up with celebrity stuff. Are you . . . doing okay?"

"It was rough at first, but I'm getting over it. Slowly."

I hesitate a moment before I ask, "Do you mind if I ask what happened? If it's too personal, don't feel obligated to tell me."

"You're fine, I promise. He had a heart attack. We were playing basketball for a charity event and . . . it happened on the court. He died in the ambulance on the way to the hospital. Holding my hand."

I don't know what to say. I can't imagine losing my dad in such an unexpected way. "I'm sorry, Jax. If there's anything I can do."

He's already shaking his head. "I'm fine. And it's okay. It takes some getting used to when you lose someone, but life goes on. And they'd want us to keep going, you know? He's the reason I quit partying. I knew he'd be disappointed. And now he can maybe, hopefully be proud of me for trying to do what's right."

I nod and swallow the lump in my throat as I think of Maddy. What would I do if I lost her? What would it feel like to wake up every morning knowing she wasn't going to be there to talk to or laugh with anymore? I shake my head at the thoughts slamming into my head and stare out the window instead. Because it's a very real possibility that it could happen. It's just a matter of time.

"I didn't make you sad, did I?"

I glance over, surprised at the amount of emotion I

can see on Jax's face. "No. You didn't make me sad. I'm so sorry you lost your dad. I was thinking about how I'd feel if I lose my sister. And I'm just nervous about . . . You know."

"You sure you're up to going right now?"

"Yes. I need to just get it over with. It's the reason I came. Even if I'm slightly regretting my decision now."

He reaches over and grabs my hand. "Everything will be okay. No matter what happens. You came here for a reason, no matter the outcome."

"I know."

He doesn't let go of my hand. And that's not a complaint.

CHAPTER 16

The only road I walk alone is the road I paved myself.
—J.S.

Jax tells the taxi driver to pull over once we reach the right neighborhood, and he does as he says. "Thanks," Jax says as he gets out of the car and pays the driver.

I swear I'm going to owe him thousands of dollars by the time I'm ready to go home.

"This is nice," I say as I get a look around. The street is charming. Apartment buildings stand on either side of the street, all different colors in the mid-day sun. I'm surprised it's such a clean street, actually. Considering all the movies I've seen that take place in what I'm assuming is another part of New York. You know—the not so great neighbor-hoods full of gangs, murder, the usual.

We walk a few paces down the street and my stomach is in knots. Maybe I shouldn't have eaten breakfast because it feels like it's going to come back up.

"This is it," Jax says, pulling me to a stop. "You ready?"

"No."

He squeezes my shoulder. "You'll be fine. Do you want me to come with you?"

I shake my head. "No. I need to go myself." I stare at the apartment building in front of me and surprise myself by taking a deep breath and starting toward it. I look over my shoulder at Jax. "I don't think I'll be too long." I want to ask him to stay and wait, but I don't want to sound needy. I think he notices my distress because his face softens.

"I'll just wait for you out here then."

I let out a relieved breath. "Thank you." I shoot him a small smile, which he returns and turn around again.

As I near the stoop, I notice the car in the driveway. A black BMW of all things. There's a little pink bike with training wheels and a bigger one without them leaning against the side of the building. Boxes of flowers line the window sills on the ground floor, all lovely and in bloom.

Everything looks so . . . normal. A normal home with normal people who ride normal bikes and drive normal— well, normal expensive—cars and live on normal streets with normal flowers in little boxes around windows.

How can someone so normal leave their husband and children and run away?

I can feel myself freaking out.

My palms are sweaty and my stomach is sick. I swallow the lump in my throat and let out a slow breath. *This is going to be fine. You're fine. Relax, Mia. She's a person, not a monster. A stranger, yes, but still. She's just a person.*

I'm shaking as I climb the three steps, walk across the porch, lift my hand, and knock on the door as though I've been here a thousand times.

It takes a second, but the door opens and an older woman stands in front of me wearing a light green apron and holding a black dishtowel. She adjusts her wire-rimmed glasses and smiles. "*Hola?*"

Say something, Mia.

"Um . . . hi. Does Carmen Santalina live here?"

"English then." The woman smiles, then shakes her head. "No. I'm afraid she doesn't." Her Spanish accent is thick and warm. Welcoming. Not at all what I was expecting.

My stomach twists and turns. I can't believe Dad gave me the wrong address. I feel like an idiot. "Oh. Sorry to bother you." I start backing away.

"My daughter lives in Queens," she says. "Wait here one minute." She disappears around the corner and I look back at Jax, who stands with his hands in his pockets on the sidewalk across the grass. I muster a tiny smile and turn back around. I hear her rummaging around her house and then she appears in the doorway again. "Here's her address." She hands me a piece of paper. "She works until five, so don't bother going over there this early. No one will be there." She looks at me, for real this time, her eyes never leaving my face. "I'm sorry, but do I know you?"

My cheeks flush. It just barely registered that this woman is my grandmother. I have another grandmother. Flesh and blood. And I've never met her before in my life. Does she know I exist? Have a clue who I am? I should tell her, especially since Dad said she was nice, but the words don't come out. I wouldn't know what to say if she started asking a bunch of questions. So I just smile and shake my head. "No. Thank you so much for your help."

The woman nods, her eyes watching me for a moment longer before she shuts the door and I hear the lock click. I hurry down the porch steps and back to Jax.

"How did it go?'

"She doesn't live here. It was her mom's house. My . . . grandmother." I hold up the paper, thankful she gave me an address so I don't have to scour the phonebooks or Internet to find her. "She gave me this, though. She said she works and doesn't get home until five."

"I'll put it in my phone and we can go track her down at five then. I don't want you to use up your data plan here." He pauses. "Did you tell her who you were?"

"No."

He nods. No questions why, just a nod.

I put the paper in my back pocket, still shaking a little from the exchange on the porch. "What am I gonna do until then?"

Jax smiles, easing my anxiety. "We'll hit the town."

"I'm not really a partier. If you couldn't tell that already."

He laughs. "I didn't mean a party. I'll take you to some of the usual tourist places so you can take a few pictures. You know. Make a few memories."

I told Maddy I'd bring her a souvenir, so this could be a good thing.

"Pretty sure I've made lots of weird memories so far."

"You're calling me weird?"

I laugh. "No, I just never thought I'd be hanging out

148

with someone famous. And a nice famous person at that. Seriously. Thank you for everything. I need to find a way to repay you. For everything."

"I won't take it, so don't worry about it."

"But—"

"Mia, I have more money than I know what to do with. And I wouldn't spend it if I didn't want to."

It would be nice to have that kind of security. I think. Still. I feel bad. He doesn't even know me very well and he's done so much for me already. Jax must see how conflicted I'm feeling because he changes the subject.

"So is there anywhere you'd like to visit while we're here?" A taxi pulls up to us and he opens the door for me. He must have called one of them while I was at Carmen's mother's house. My *grandmother's* house. I still can't get over knowing that fact—and that I simply walked away without telling her who I was. I guess I had a good teacher.

"Hmmm . . . Central Park, I suppose? I've always wanted to go there. The pictures I've seen are beautiful. And it's across from the hotel, so if I need to go back and rev myself up before I go see my birth mom, I can do that." I climb inside and he shuts the door before walking around behind the taxi to get in the other side. Once he closes the door, he tells the cabby where to go.

"Central Park it is. I know the perfect part to walk through. Did you want to see Ground Zero?"

"Oh, I've always wanted to go to Ground Zero."

"Done."

"Thank you for being my tour guide."

"I wouldn't want to be anywhere else." His phone rings and he pulls it out of his pocket. He looks at the caller, frowns, and lets it finish ringing.

"Sorry," he says as his phone beeps. He pushes a button before putting the phone next to his ear. Listening to a message, I assume. A voice yells on the other end. I can't understand what the man is saying, but the look on Jax's face tells me it can't be good.

He frowns as the message ends and puts the phone back in his pocket when he's done. "My manager." He scowls at the ground.

I sit in my seat for a second, waiting for him to say something else, but he doesn't. "Your manager? Do you need to call him back?"

He shakes his head. "Not right now. I'll give him a bit to cool down. Then I'll call. It would probably be best for you to not be next to me." He grins. "On account of sensitive ears."

I laugh out loud at that one. "Thanks for thinking about my well-being while you're focusing on your career." I frown. "You're not going to get fired or anything, are you?"

"Ha!"

"I take that as a no."

"He won't fire me."

"You're sure you won't be in trouble? I'll plug my ears if you really need to call him back."

He grins. "I'm fine. Promise. Like I said before, I'll do

it later. I know what I want to do and I'm going to do it. Thanks to you."

"Okay," I say, still not convinced. "What did I do?"

"You told me I should follow my dreams. And you're right. So I'm going to."

"I don't want you to get in trouble because of it, though."

"I'll work it out. Promise."

"Okay . . ." I bite my lip.

He chuckles. "Seriously. No worries. Today I just want to enjoy hanging out with a nice girl. I don't want to worry about life. Know what I mean?"

"Yes. I really do." Not worrying about things? I wish. Maddy's the only thing I've worried about for the last two years. I don't know how to not worry. But after tonight, hopefully—maybe—I won't have to worry too much longer. Carmen will save Maddy and I'll finally have my sister back.

If my plan doesn't work, I don't know what I'll do.

"If you don't want to hang out with me, though, tell me and I'll take you back to the hotel. You know, if I'm bugging you or . . . I don't know. I'm basically a stranger to you, but I swear I'm a nice stranger."

"From what I've already seen, I'm not worried. And I don't consider you a stranger at all anymore. I know your deep, dark secrets. We're friends."

He meets my eyes. "Good." His little grin is back and he looks away, his cheeks pink. He clears his throat. "Let me know when you're hungry. I have the perfect place to take you to lunch."

"Oh?"

"One bite at this place and you'll never want to leave New York."

I glance at him as he pulls his baseball cap down and leans against the seat. He looks so normal. Like he's just an average teenager, out on the town with a friend. But he's not just an average teen. He's a rockstar. Famous. And I'm already trying to figure out how long it will take for people to recognize him before our day is over.

Not very long, I'm guessing. But for now, I'll enjoy spending time with him. Until I see Carmen for the first time in fifteen years.

It's kind of scary that my sister's fate rests in her hands. But I have a feeling everything will work itself out. It has to.

CHAPTER 17

Music is therapeutic; lyrics are healing.
Put them together and you might just find yourself again.
—*J.S.*

Central Park is amazing. I know I've seen it in the movies several times, but that's nothing compared to the real thing. It's seriously huge. There's no way I'd be able to see everything in one day. No way.

I've already seen a guy on a unicycle, a beatboxing duo, a group of about eighty people doing yoga on the grass, random sun bathers in bikinis, and a mini female orchestra playing songs for people who pass by.

"You like it?"

I glance at Jax and grin. "Love it. This place is so alive. So many interesting people. Plus, everything's so green." I glance up at the huge trees creating a canopy above us. "Oh, that bridge over there is so cute. It reminds me of a fairytale."

"A fairytale, huh?"

I nod and shove my hands in my pockets, breathing in the fresh air. I could live somewhere like this. Not in the big city, but having access to this amazing park would be heaven. "Don't you believe in fairytales?"

He shrugs and pulls down his cap as a group of girls walk by. "I've never really thought about it."

"You should. I guess some are kind of disturbing. Hansel and Gretel and the cannibal witch kind of freaked me out as a child, but the happily-ever-afters get me every time."

He groans. "Not the princess ones."

"Those are the best. I do love a girl hero story, but I love a good knight in shining armor saving the princess tale, too. Call me old-fashioned. I don't care."

"Nothing wrong with that."

"I'm a nerd, I know."

He chuckles and we walk in comfortable silence for a while. A group of runners pass us by and I wish I had my running gear. If I actually had running gear. I know it's just like running anywhere, but Central Park makes it seem so much cooler. I'd totally be a runner here. Maybe even a marathon runner.

Then again . . . maybe I should just settle for running one mile without passing out first. In soccer, at least I get a small break sometimes.

We pass a guy with a guitar singing a soulful song. It's beautiful and I wish I had some money with me to put in his guitar case. All I have are credit cards. I stop anyway, and we listen to him sing for a few minutes. I nudge Jax with my elbow. "You should do this sometime."

"Believe me, I would if I knew I wouldn't get mobbed." He glances around. "Which . . . may be happening, by the way."

"What?"

"See that tree over there?"

I glance to where he's motioning with his head. "Yeah . . . ?" It takes me a minute, but then I see a person poke his head around with a phone pointed in our direction. I know he's snapping pictures of us. "I didn't think they'd find us so quick, but obviously I was wrong."

"There's more than one?"

"Always. Come on." Jax grabs my hand and starts walking back in the direction we came from. Not rushing me, but not slow either.

We pass a group of teenagers who obviously recognize Jax and whisper as they take pictures on their phones. They don't approach, but giggle as we walk by.

"Excuse us," Jax says as he moves through a small crowd watching some street performer, I assume. I can't see what's going on, so I focus on Jax instead. People move out of our way. Some seem to recognize him, some don't. Most ignore us completely, which for his sake, is nice. I squeeze his hand hard so I don't lose him and he squeezes back.

"Will you really get mobbed?" I ask.

"Probably not here. People normally keep their distance and leave me alone, but there are always a few who like to chase."

Just then, a man with dark hair and really white skin matches our pace and holds a mini camcorder up to Jax's face. It's the man who was behind the tree. "Jaxton, are you still fighting with the rest of your band? Is that why you're in New York and the other three are still in L.A.? Are the rumors true? Are you breaking up?"

155

Jax doesn't even look at him, just keeps his eyes straight ahead and pulls me closer to him.

"Who's the mystery girl? Is she from around here? Are you on a date? Are you two secretly dating?"

"Sorry, no questions today," Jax says. It's polite, but there's an edge to his voice that says *leave me alone*. The guy backs off a little, but it doesn't stop a woman from taking his place. There are two of them now. Following, talking nonstop as we walk toward the street.

We're walking fast. Almost faster than my short legs can keep up with. We pass a few runners, a few families with kids. Most people seem to recognize him but stay back at a respectful distance. Some take pictures with their phones, but others just watch, curious.

The man and the woman won't give up so quick.

The woman appears on my side and shoves her phone in my face. I'm assuming the microphone is recording.

"Are you and Jaxton a couple? What's your name? How long have you been together?"

I'm feeling claustrophobic. I can't do anything but stare at her with my mouth opening and closing.

Breathe, Mia.

Jax pulls me behind him and to his other side, thankfully getting me away from her. Then she starts into him. "Hey, Jaxton, what's going on with Blue Fire? Is it true you're taking a break and starting a solo career? Who's the mystery girl you're with? Give us a name."

The man who's been following us asks, "Jaxton, is Blue Fire really on the verge of a breakup?"

Jax ignores him as well and heads toward the street where a bunch of taxis wait. We can't get there soon enough.

The woman gives up on Jax and comes to my side again. "What's your name? Are you dating? What about Melanie Price? What does she feel about this?"

"Have you had anymore stints in rehab?" I hear the man ask Jax. "Is this girl your rebound from Melanie Price?"

Jax doesn't react or respond, other than hurrying me toward the closest taxi. He opens the back door of one and I hurry to scoot over as he joins me inside.

The paparazzi are peppering him with questions even as he rolls up the window and he tells the cabby where to take us.

We leave both of them on the curb as we drive away.

That was awful.

I let out a breath of relief and glance at Jax. He leans his head back and squeezes his eyes shut. He looks exhausted. I can't imagine living like that every single day. Having to watch out for people wherever you go. Worrying about people taking pictures of you, even when all you're doing is going for a walk. I feel bad for him. And what they said about him. Rehab? Was that true? Or was it just something to put in the tabloids to get a reaction from fans?

And I wonder about Melanie Price, as well.

"I'm sorry," I whisper. I reach out and take his hand. I don't know what else to do. I'm surprised when he squeezes it back.

"Don't *you* be sorry. *I* should be the one apologizing.

157

Not you. I'm sorry you got roped into all this. Usually people aren't super aggressive like that. Usually only when there's a bit of drama with the band. Which there is right now." He opens his eyes and looks down at me. I didn't realize we were sitting so close to each other until now. I don't even have my seatbelt on, which is very rebellious of me. I pull it on. "I just want to warn you," Jax says. "There will probably be pictures in magazines of you now. And there will definitely be a bunch on the Internet. I apologize in advance."

I shrug. "There are worse things that could happen." I could have looked like I did yesterday. At least I have makeup on and my hair's done today. "Actually, if my parents see it before I get home, I'll have to explain myself. Hanging out with a rockstar. What was I thinking?" I reach up and pull the brim of his hat down, trying to cover his eyes.

He catches my hand and grins, his blue eyes holding mine. He doesn't let go and I, for some reason, can't remember my name. I'm starting to have feelings. And feelings aren't good. Especially when it comes to crushing on someone I can't ever have.

He's so . . . good. He's funny and kind and has been nothing but selfless since I arrived in New York. Who helps a random girl get a hotel room and show her around the city just because? A kind, normal, and respectful guy. And there's no way *I'm* good enough for someone like him.

I move my hand and fold my arms across my chest. "So, where to now?"

He smiles, but it doesn't quite reach his eyes. I don't know if it was a sign of rejection or what. Like he'd be sad if I rejected him. He could get any girl in the world. What do I mean to someone like him? At the end of the day, nothing.

"Lunch. I figured we just got some exercise outrunning the paparazzi, so how about some pizza?"

"That sounds great. But I'm buying."

He shakes his head. "You'll never learn."

"I learn something new every day. Like how to escape a bunch of cameras coming toward my face."

"We need to learn some ninja skills."

"For real. I'm sure I could bust some out."

He laughs. "I'd love to see that."

I catch the cabby rolling his eyes in the rear-view, but I don't mind. I love having someone to be nerdy with.

Never would have guessed it would end up being Jaxton Scott, though.

CHAPTER 18

Memories haunt your fragile mind
Step out of your skin, leave your troubles behind.
We all have our baggage, our bruises and scars
Stay with me tonight and we'll scatter the stars
—J.S.

The pizza place is nicer than I expected. You know. Because it's a pizza place.

We seat ourselves near the back and I pick up the menu that sits on the table. I skim it for a second before getting distracted by the decor and ambiance.

An old piano sits in the corner with a sign that says PLAY ME and my fingers itch to do just that. I refrain, though. I don't know anyone here and I don't know if I could perform on a whim like that. I turn my attention elsewhere. Names of celebrities line the walls with their signatures signed on napkins and displayed in picture frames. They're all around the room. Kind of a cute idea. And holy crap they have a lot. This must be some amazing pizza indeed.

"Are you up there?" I nod toward the frames, and Jax smiles and points to one clear across the room. BLUE FIRE is in huge letters along the top of the wall and photos of Jax and the three other members of the band are all lined up in a row underneath. "Figures you'd be one of the biggest names in here."

All he does is shrug as the waiter comes over to our table. "Hello, Mr. Scott. The usual today?"

The corner of my mouth twitches. I swear he knows everyone.

Jax doesn't look at his menu at all, just leans toward me. "Is ham and pineapple okay?"

My stomach growls. I'd eat anything at this point, but ham and pineapple is coincidentally my favorite. "Yes."

The waiter smiles, sticks a pen behind his ear, and disappears into the back.

"You come here often?" I ask.

"Best pizza in Manhattan."

"I'll be the judge of that."

He laughs. "Of course. But I can't wait to see your face when you taste it. It's awesome."

"Challenge accepted."

He glances toward the piano and nods at it. "So, how 'bout a dare."

"What kind of dare?"

"I dare you to play that."

"Um, I don't think so."

"Why not?"

My stomach twists. "I don't want to bother everyone."

"You won't bother anyone. That's what it's there for. And from the way you talked about the piano on the plane, I assume you play well."

161

"I wouldn't say well . . ."

"How long have you been playing?"

"A while."

"As in . . . A year? Two?"

"Thirteen."

Before I know what's happening, he's pulling me out of the booth and across the room. He sits me down and opens the piano, exposing chipped and yellowed keys. "Play."

"Jax . . ."

"Thirteen years? Come on. That's like forever. You have to know at least one song. Didn't your teacher make you memorize any?"

I want to humor him and play chopsticks or something easy like that, but I can't bring myself to do that. Instead, I stare at the keys as my fingers find the right notes by themselves. "Okay. Maybe just a little song." I smile, happy to be in my zone for a moment, and pretend no one but Jax is in the room. I decide on one of my favorites, "Maple Leaf Rag," and the second I start playing, people behind me start clapping along and hollering.

My fingers fly over the keys as the music fills the restaurant, and Jax just stands there, leaning next to the edge of the piano, tapping his hand on the wood. I don't look at him. I can feel his stare, but I'm so invested in my song that it doesn't really bother me for once.

By the time I come to the end of my song, the piano is surrounded by people. I see cameras flashing, which is weird, I swear I'm not that good, but then I remember Jax is here and people know him.

I end with a fun glissando of my own making and a loud chord at the end. The chord echoes through the room, and when I take my fingers off the keys, the room explodes in applause.

My face is bright red, I'm sure, but as Jax grabs my hand and tells me to take a bow, I oblige. I've never been so . . . flattered before. I do a little curtsey before beelining it to our booth again.

I sit down and put my face in my hands, but I'm all smiles.

"That was amazing," Jax said. "I didn't know you were that good."

I shrug. "I'm not."

"Right." He cracks a smile. "But seriously. I could feel the electricity coming off you as you played that piano. You love it."

I nod, the adrenaline still flowing through my veins, making me feel higher than I have in a long time. "I do."

The waiter comes over and sets the pizza down on the table. "That was amazing, miss. We don't have people play very often. Too afraid to show their talents. Well done. Be sure to visit us again." He nods at me and walks away.

I'm not really sure what to say now but I'm grateful for his words. It makes me realize how much I love music. How much I'd love to play professionally. Not to the extent of being famous, but being in the background doing what I love would be awesome.

Jax grabs a slice of pizza and puts it on his plate. He gestures for me to do the same. "Ready to fall in love?"

I stare at him as he takes a bite of his slice. He's so cute as he closes his eyes like he's just eaten the best thing on earth. "Heaven," he says before taking another bite.

"Oh, fine. Let me try it." I pick up a slice and bite off the tip and am greeted with an explosion of spices in my mouth. Delicious. I exaggerate a sigh, just for his benefit, and start laughing.

He rolls his eyes. "Very funny. But for real. Do you like it?"

I have to agree. It's amazing. "It's awesome. Best pizza I've ever tasted."

"Really?" He gives me a skeptical look.

"Really. Thanks for showing me this little piece of Heaven." I sigh. "Maddy would love this place."

"You can bring her someday." He says it so matter-of-factly that I really wish it were possible. And maybe it still can be. After tonight, I'll know. "Does she play the piano like you?"

"No. She actually plays the violin."

"Ah. I like the violin. When it can be played well. Not when it sounds like your ears are being scratched out."

I almost spit water out of my mouth. "Agreed. She's really good, though. First chair in her high school orchestra."

"Awesome."

"We've done a few duets. I love playing with her."

We sit in comfortable silence as we finish our food. By the time the pizza is halfway gone, we're both stuffed.

"I wish we could get a to-go box, but we're not going to be by a fridge anytime soon."

Jax nods. "You ready to go?"

"Yep." As he pays the waiter, I take a good look around this wonderful little place again. At the old, worn piano that has a crisp sound even though some of the keys are chipped and cracked. Places like this may be old and worn, but they're still worth something. And from all the napkins lining the walls, it's clear that a lot of people think the same thing.

"Off to see Ground Zero." Jax takes my hand and laces his fingers through mine. He looks down at me, making sure it's okay, and all I can do is smile and nod as he leads me to the door.

CHAPTER 19

I want to be clean, I want to heal
Emptiness is all I'll ever feel.
—J.S.

It's so quiet here. Even with the noise of traffic in the background, Ground Zero has a different feel. Peaceful. Silent. I think of all the men and women who died that day as I run my fingers over the black stone engraved with all the names that surround the pools. So many names. Still so hard to comprehend what that day must have been like at this very spot.

I can't even imagine.

Jax gives my hand a gentle squeeze and leads me to the next one, through the beautiful green trees planted all around the memorial. I don't know how this place could be any more breathtaking, but when the trees are huge and full grown, it will be.

We reach the next pool and I study some of the names in the stone. I don't know these people, but they're a part of me. They're a part of everyone, I think, and I know they're watching over their loved ones from up above.

"It's hard to think about, huh?" he says as he stares into the pool.

"Yeah." I glance at a group of people walking quietly around the pool. Some reach out and touch the names, some just fold their arms and stare. It's interesting how different people react to things.

I watch how the water slides down the black stone and into the fountain. I love that they made the memorial like this. With the water always moving, always flowing. It makes me realize how resilient our country is. How hopeful we are. How we're able to keep moving forward even when bad things knock us down.

We're all made that way, I think. Some of us have to search deeper than others when things get us down, but that spark of hope that keeps us going when life gets hard is always there. It's somewhere inside all of us, even when we think we've lost it.

It's all I can count on when I think of my sister.

We walk slowly around, me touching the names, Jax with his hands in his pockets. When he speaks again, I jump. "So, I'm curious," he says. "If your mom . . . or . . . That woman tonight doesn't want to donate a kidney to your sister, what are you going to do?"

I don't want to think about that. But I have to. It's a huge possibility. "I guess I'll just start over. Look for someone else who can."

"And if you can't find anyone then?"

I fold my arms and let out a slow breath. "Then I help

her fight until she can't anymore. I know she'll be okay . . . whatever happens."

He nods. "You're pretty amazing, you know that?"

"Not really."

"You love her. That's obvious. But I have a feeling you'd do this for anyone. Friends, parents, other siblings."

"Yes. I would. My family is very close, so I'd definitely do anything for them. My dad had a lot on his plate after Carmen left, and he's been there for me like no one else has. Came to every piano recital, every soccer game when I was little. It didn't matter what it was. He has always supported me and has always been there. And my mom, too. When she married my dad, she was wonderful. I know a lot of people don't get along with their step-parents, but my mom is the best mom I could ever have asked for. She's helped me through so many things."

I swallow, getting emotional for some reason. I never thought about how much she's been involved in my life and how lucky I am to have such supportive parents. They mean everything to me. I need to tell them that when I get home. I don't tell them enough, if at all.

He shakes his head. "You're amazing. Doing so much to save your sister."

"Wouldn't you? If you had the chance to save someone's life, wouldn't you take it?"

"I definitely would." He sighs. "But I have to save myself first."

He doesn't elaborate and I don't push him. I glance up at him, seeing the tortured look on his face. There's something there. Some darkness trying to find its way out. Instead of asking if he's okay, I link my arm with his and we just enjoy our time together, both of us lost in thoughts we don't really want in our heads.

"So, tell me about your mom," I say.

My phone rings as I walk, and as I see the name on the caller ID, I smile.

"Maddy?" I almost yell. "Hey! Are you okay?"

"Hey," she says. Her voice is almost a whisper. "I just . . . when are you coming home?"

I push down the panic that creeps through my body. "Soon. Why? What's wrong?" I try to keep my voice neutral so she won't hear the worry.

She's quiet a moment before she continues. "Mia, I don't think I have very much longer. The doctors say there's nothing more they can do unless I get a donor." I bite my lip, fighting the tears filling my eyes. "I'm okay with it. But I just . . . I need you with me when it's time. You know. For me to go. And I'm pretty sure it's close. My body isn't cooperating anymore."

"Don't give up, Maddy. Please." My voice cracks on the last word and I glance at Jax, who watches me, understanding.

"They're going to try some new medication to see if that changes anything. I'll let you know how it goes."

"I'm sure it will be fine."

She's quiet. "Just come home soon, okay? Have you seen Carmen yet?"

"No. A few more hours."

"Good luck. I'd be freaking out if I were you."

"Believe me. I am." I clear my throat, "I'll get a flight as soon as possible, okay?"

"Okay." I hear her let out a sigh of relief. "I'll see you soon."

"Love you," I say.

"Love you, too."

I stare at her picture on my phone before it disappears.

"Everything okay?" Jax asks.

I shake my head. "I have to go see Carmen now." I check the time on my phone. It's almost five. I blink back tears and fight to keep my emotions under control. There will be time to cry later.

"Let's go then."

My fingers find his, as if they knew I'd need some kind of lifeline to help me put one foot in front of the other, and we walk back to the street, past the pools of names and families still grieving over their lost loved ones.

I don't want to grieve over someone so close. This idea of mine has to work. Carmen will understand.

She has to understand.

CHAPTER 20

People aren't always what they seem.
Even when you think they are.
—J.S.

This street is more like the movies I've seen. More deserted, not as happy, kind of scary. A few people stand outside the apartment complex and I'm getting this sudden urge to stay in the cab.

"This is it," Jax says.

The cab pulls over and a few people standing around on the sidewalk glance over at us. Jax opens the door and gets out as I force myself to slide across the seat to do the same. He tips the cab driver and I watch as he drives away without us.

We're stuck in this place and who knows if we'll be able to catch another cab. What if we're stuck here all night?

Jax sets a hand on my back and leans toward me. "You ready? We should probably move."

I glance around, feeling very out of place. And very overwhelmed. My real mother is somewhere in this apartment complex and has no idea I'm standing outside. I start toward the door and try to open it, but it's locked. "What do we do?"

"Have someone buzz us in, or wait for someone to come out and make them believe we live here."

Who knows how long that will take. I sigh, defeated. "Great."

"You okay?"

I'm shaking. I didn't realize it before, but I can feel my body trembling now. "Huh? Oh. Um . . . Yes." I rub at the goosebumps rippling across my arms. I can't stop thinking about Maddy's phone call. If she wants me to come home that bad, she must be getting worse. I have to book a flight tonight. As soon as possible.

Jax looks at the names of the people living in the apartment listed by an intercom attached to the wall. "Carmen Santalina?"

"Yes. That's her."

"She's in 5B. Should I buzz her to let us in?"

I'm not sure what to do. Should I push the intercom button and tell her who I am? Would she even let me in? I turn and stare at the red brick building. It's old, that's for sure, but it doesn't look too bad on the outside. A little scary, yes, but not bad. Hopefully it's not scary inside.

"Should I buzz her then?" Jax asks.

"I don't know." I can feel peoples' eyes on us as we stand in front of the doors. We really should get inside. It's getting sketchy out here. "Jax, look."

A man walks toward the door from the inside, and when he opens it, he bumps into me. Jax pulls me out of the way and catches the door as the grumpy man brushes past us and onto the street. "Thanks," Jax says to the man, but he doesn't even look at him. Just gives me an annoyed look instead.

I'm expecting the man to turn around and stop us from going inside, but he doesn't. All he does is mutter something under his breath and walks away.

"Well, that was easy," I say.

We're standing inside now and I'm staring down the hall. I try to tell my feet to move, but they don't. I can't. Jax's fingers find mine and I let him lead me down the hall and up five flights of stairs.

"Do you want me to come with you this time?"

"What?" My mind is everywhere.

Jax squeezes my hand and I make myself focus on him. "Do you want me to come with you? You look like you're gonna throw up or something."

"I feel like I'm going to." I give him a shaky smile. "And no. I'm okay. I'll go in myself." I think. I hope. We'll see.

"Okay." We stop in front of 5B. "I'll be right outside if you need me."

"You don't have to—"

"Mia. This is New York. And by the time you get out of here, it will be dark. I don't care how stubborn or brave you think you are. There's no way I'm letting you walk back out of this apartment complex by yourself."

I want to argue, but I'm too on edge to do anything but nod.

Jax squeezes my hand again before letting go. "It's okay. It will be fine. Take a deep breath and knock on the door."

I can do that. Knock on the door. I'm not sure if I can stand here and wait for someone to answer, but at least I can knock, right?

I twist my hands together and stare at the door, expecting it to open by itself. It doesn't. I want to run away right now. I shouldn't be here, I should be at home with Maddy. With my brother and my parents. But I have to do this. I have to save Maddy. And Carmen is the only one who can help me now.

She's her only chance.

What do I look like? A mess? I pull my elastic out of my hair and let my dark hair fall around my shoulders. I glance at Jax. "Do I look horrible? Tell me the truth please."

He's staring at me as I shake my hair out again, his mouth half open. He swallows. "Um . . . no. Far from it."

"Oh. Okay." That makes me feel a little better, but he could just be lying to be nice. He doesn't seem like the lying type, though.

After I smooth my hair down and roll my shoulders to get the tension out, I think I'm ready.

My body trembles as I lift my right hand to the door. I knock. It's small, but enough to be heard, I think. Footsteps sound. A child yells something in the background and I hear running feet.

I take a deep breath as the door opens.

And I'm staring into the face of a girl.

A girl who looks like Maddy.

CHAPTER 21

Words mean nothing to those who don't listen.
They bounce off them, not leaving a mark and end up dying in
the wind.
Listen.
—J.S.

I'm so startled, all I can do is stare at her.

"*Como te puedo ayudar?*" The girl looks at me expect-antly, waiting for me to say something. She's younger, I'd guess twelve maybe. She has darker skin than mine, but there's no doubt she's related. Her and Maddy could be twins. Their small noses, thin lips, dark eyes. She could be a cousin, but I have a feeling she's much more than that.

"*Hola?*"

I swear my mouth works. My voice, too. But when I try to say something coherent, all that comes out is, "Uh . . ." I shake my head, trying to tell her I don't understand. Even though I do know she said hello. That's about all the Spanish I know.

The girl smiles. "Oh. English?"

I nod, relieved my brain is sort of working again. "Is, um, Carmen here?"

"Yes, she is. Just a minute." Her accent is thick, her voice musical and bright. She gestures for me to come inside and I follow her, taking one last glance at Jax before she shuts the door. "Mama! There's someone here to see you!"

Mama. This girl is my sister. Half-sister, but blood-related. I have another sister. I wonder if Dad knows she had another child. How many other children does she have?

I hear a shout from somewhere in the back of the apartment, but my attention is on the woman standing in the doorway of what I think is the kitchen. She holds a dishtowel in her hand and stares. I know she's not my mother, but she looks like her just the same. Looks like me. The dark brown hair, tanned skin, chocolate eyes. Her mouth drops open when she sees me and she puts a hand to her chest. I watch her walk across the room toward me, her eyes never leaving my face.

"Your name? What is your name, child?"

The look on her face makes me take a step back. "Mia?"

"Mia," she whispers before covering her mouth with both her hands. "You're Mia?"

I nod.

"Clary, who is it?"

My breath catches as the woman who gave birth to me speaks from behind the woman with the dishtowel. She's in a bright red dress with heels of all things as she walks across the living room toward me. She's beautiful. No wonder Dad was so smitten with her. When she sees me, her perfect eyebrows raise and she touches her lips with her manicured nails as her eyes grow wide. We stare at each other, a million questions running through my head, none of which I'm ready to ask.

The girl who answered the door comes running in the room and stands next to Carmen, a question in her eyes. "Mama?"

"*Dejame un momento.*" She touches the girl's hair, her eyes never leaving mine. The girl glances at me once before going in the other room.

"Carmen, this is—"

Carmen glances at her sister. At least, I think it's her sister. My aunt. "I know who this is, Ana. Could you give us a moment please?"

Ana gives me a fleeting look before retreating into the other room.

To say the tension in the room is super awkward is an understatement. This woman, my mother, is not some happy, kind person. I can tell how cold she is by the way she carries herself. Not smiling, stiff, no feeling in her dark eyes. So different than what I imagined. As I look at her up close, I can see hard lines in her features, making her look older than I originally thought. Like she's been through her share of hardships.

"Have a seat, Mia," Carmen says. She gestures toward a flowery couch, but I don't move. I can't believe she's just standing there staring at me. You'd think she'd rush over to me, wrap me in a hug, and apologize for leaving me so many years earlier. But she doesn't. She walks calmly past me and sits on the couch, her hands folded neatly in her lap, waiting for me to do the same.

After standing there like an idiot, I turn around and sit on the couch facing her.

I don't know where to look. Anywhere but at her, I'm thinking. So I settle on the floor. Or, I guess her shoes. Her red heels, which I swear are taller than me.

"Did your father send you to find me?" Her voice is low. Quiet. Kind of intimidating.

"No!" I answer too quick, but at least it's the truth. I take a deep breath, trying to keep my cool. "No. He didn't even know I was coming."

She nods. "How is he? Your father."

"He's good. Really good. Married and happy."

She nods again, not saying a word. So much nodding.

The silence is overwhelming. Crushing, actually. This reunion is not going well at all. It's nothing like I imagined it would be. It's nothing like any reunion with a long-lost parent should be. And I want to cry. But instead of doing that, I cut right to the chase. She seems like she's a blunt person, so I hurry and tell her why I'm here. "Look. Carmen." I say her name and it sounds so foreign coming off my tongue that I shake my head when it comes out. "The reason I'm here is because of Maddy."

"Oh?"

"She's dying."

I expect her to react. To do anything other than sit there. To show some degree of emotion I craved from a mother as a child. But she does nothing but disappoint me. Her dark eyes search me over and she sweeps her dark hair behind her shoulder. "What's wrong with her?"

"She has kidney failure. I thought I could donate one of mine to her, but I'm not a match. I was wondering . . ." I trail off. How do I put this into words without sounding like I want to use her for her kidneys? "I was wondering if there was any way you could . . ."

"Let me guess. You want me to donate one of my kidneys to her?"

The way she says it makes my whole body tense. Calm, but clipped and annoyed. "Yes."

She sits there a moment, staring at her hands. Then she looks at me. Something like regret flashes across her face, but it's gone just as fast. "You know, I didn't want to leave you girls when you were little. I was young. I was scared. Scared to be a mother and give up the next twenty or so years to raising you."

I stare at her and wait for her to speak again. She doesn't. So I do. "But you left us anyway."

She hesitates, but nods. "It wasn't supposed to happen like that. I was happy with one child. You were a good baby. Not too overwhelming. But when Maddy was born? I couldn't handle it. I was going to take you with me and just leave Maddy."

My heart feels like it's being torn out of my chest. What would have happened if I never had Maddy to grow up with? I can't imagine.

"But I didn't have money to get us both back across the country to my family. Besides, your father was smitten with both of you. He thought it best to leave you together."

I've never loved Dad more than I do at this very moment. Bless that man.

"I'm sorry. I really am, but it was for the best. And we've been fine living our separate lives all these years. All of us moving on. Leaving the past in the past and not worrying about old mistakes."

Mistakes. So that's all Maddy and I are to her. Mistakes. I frown. "But Maddy's disease isn't in the past. It's happening right now."

She sighs. "I'm not her mother anymore, Mia. I didn't raise her at all. I know I gave birth to her, but she never called me mom."

"But I did." She opens her mouth, then closes it again. "Or did you forget that I was three when you left? Do you know how many nights I cried for my mother and you never came?"

"You can't remember that. You were too young."

"Yes. I was young when you left. But Dad can remember every single moment of those few years."

She sighs. "Mia, there are things . . . I just—"

"I had anxiety attacks as a child. I still have them. They started a few weeks after you left me." I stare at the wall, not her. "But you wouldn't know that, because you never called. Did you know Maddy is the kindest person you'll ever have the privilege of meeting? Of course you don't know that. You would know things about us if you at least tried. Tried to get to know your own *daughters*. You would know I love listening to music and how well I play the piano. You would know how much I love to watch the lightning and listen to the thunder when it rains. You would know I'm on my school's soccer team. That I would give my *life* for my sister. Because she's *family*.

I meet her eyes, but she shakes her head.

"But you wouldn't know that because you didn't care enough to check up on me. No phone calls. No letters. Nothing." I don't mean to start talking about me, but it just comes out. All the twisted feelings I've had since getting here, being in the same city as the woman who left me, are pouring out and I can't stop them. It's terrifying and liberating at the same time.

"Mia . . ."

I change the subject. "That girl. The one who answered the door. She's your daughter, isn't she?" I stare hard at her, daring her to look away. She stares back at me, and after a second gives a slight nod. "How old is she?"

"Thirteen."

I let that sink in. I have a half sister. I've had one all these years and never knew. "Do I have any other siblings I don't know about floating around in the world somewhere?"

She shakes her head. "No. I just have Clarissa."

"And her dad?"

She shakes her head. "Not important. Not anymore."

So she loved him and left him, too, I assume. Makes sense, considering her history with Dad. "Well, I'm glad you realized she was important enough for you to keep."

"That's not fair."

"And abandoning your first two daughters is?"

She bites her lip and looks at her watch like she's in a hurry to be somewhere. "I didn't have a choice."

"You did have a choice. You had three people in your life who loved you. You could have taken us with you. Dad would have gone with you. We could have been a family."

She's shaking her head before I even finish. "Your Dad and I were having problems before you were born. It's a miracle we lasted as long as we did. We disagreed over a lot of things. Too many things."

"Obviously." I'm not sure what to think of this new information, though. Dad's never really talked about it, but wouldn't he tell me they fought a lot? Maybe he wanted to spare me the details. Now I kind of wish he'd told me. It would have prepared me a little more for what she had to say.

Something sits in the back of my mind and I bite my lip before I say it. I have to know. "Did you ever think about us? At all?"

She hesitates, twisting her hands in her lap. "I'll admit I did at times. I do regret what I did back then, but so many years have gone by. I've moved on. Your father has moved on. You've moved on."

"But if you could do something to save your daughter's life after all these years, would you do it?"

"I told you before. She's not my daughter."

"But—"

"I might have been a mother to *you* once, and I'm sorry for all the pain I caused you, but I was never a mother to Madison. I held her once. We didn't bond. There was no connection between us. I was never a mother to her at all. She's a stranger to me and she has no recollection of me either. I don't owe her anything."

"That doesn't matter." Tears sting my eyes, and I fight to keep them from spilling over. I don't realize I'm standing until I've taken a step toward her. "She's your daughter. Your blood. No matter what you say, she's your *family*!"

She stands. "She's *your* family." She gives me a sad smile. "I'm sorry you came all this way for nothing."

It takes me a second to recover from the crushing blow of rejection, but I gather my wits and let my anger take over. "I'm glad I came. Now I know I can throw away that stupid birthday card you sent me when I was three years old. I can sleep at night knowing you've been raising another daughter without any thought of your other two miles and miles away." I clench my fists. "Do you have any idea how much your daughter looks like Maddy? What would you do if she were in the same position?"

She frowns. "I'd give my life to save hers."

"But you won't give a kidney to save Maddy."

She stares at me a long time before looking away and walking toward the door. "I'm sorry." As she reaches for the handle, my temper finally breaks.

"No. *I'm* sorry. I'm sorry you turned out to be exactly what I thought you were. Heartless and cold, not caring about anyone but yourself. Dad was right. I shouldn't have come."

"Mia."

I push past her. "Don't bother letting me out. I've done just fine my entire life without any help from you." I don't look at her again. All I can do is open the door, let myself out, and slam it shut.

Jax stands on the landing at the top of the steps, waiting for me. I stand there, breathing hard, my eyes filling with tears. He tries to reach out, but I push his hand away and start down the stairs.

"Mia," he says.

A sob escapes my throat. "Don't!"

I hear him following me, but I don't stop. I run. I push the apartment door open and take off down the street, tears blurring my vision. I have no idea where I'm going, no idea what I'm going to do now.

I failed.

"Mia, stop!" Jax yells as he catches up with me. He grabs my arm, pulling me to a stop. I pull away.

"Take me back to the hotel."

"Mia, what—"

"Please! I just have to get out of here." I wipe my angry tears away and force myself to calm down, staring hard at the sidewalk.

Before I know it, he's called a cab.

When it pulls up, he opens the door for me and I climb in. He gets in after me.

"Are you okay?" he asks after he tells the cabby where to go.

"No."

He doesn't say anything, just reaches over and finds my

hand. I take it. It's comforting. But I don't want to talk yet. And he doesn't push me,

He squeezes my hand to let me know he's there as I find myself staring out the window at nothing, saying nothing as we head back to my borrowed hotel room, all the while thinking two things:

Carmen was Maddy's last hope, and she won't help us.

My beautiful baby sister is going to die.

CHAPTER 22

The music flows freely, pulses through her veins
A haunting melody, bound in chains.
Her fingers glide over black and white keys
A song chilling the soft, warm breeze
—*J.S.*

I'm surprised it's not raining. Isn't it supposed to rain during the climax of a story?

But this isn't a story. This isn't a dream. All of this . . . This nightmare of epic proportions. It's real. So real, in fact, that I can't figure out what is happening to me.

I've been lying on the couch, curled in a ball, for hours. I haven't cried again. Not since before Jax called that cab. I've heard nothing from my family, nothing from Jax since he dropped me off at my room after I told him I needed to be alone. Which was stupid. I don't want to be alone. But I guess, sometimes, it's good to be alone for a while.

All I do is stare out the huge window, wondering where everything went wrong. My sister is going to die. She's going to die and there's nothing I can do about it. I knew it could happen but didn't think it would. I always had hope. Now I have to face the fact that there's nothing left for her unless she moves to the top of the donor list. But it's unlikely that will happen. What will I do without Maddy? What will I do when I walk past her room and realize she'll never be practicing her violin again or begging me to watch some celebrity news show with her? Who will I talk to when I'm having a bad day or when I finish a good book and need to gush about it with someone?

It's a lot to take in. A lot to think about. I don't want to think about it.

My stomach growls. I haven't had dinner, but I can't bring myself to do anything but lie here.

I jump as someone knocks on my door. I lie there a moment longer but finally make myself stand before I shuffle over to the door. I glance out the peephole and see Jax.

I hesitate only a second before I open the door.

I must look like a complete freak show. He doesn't seem to notice, however, as he closes the distance between us and wraps me in a hug.

That's when the tears come.

He doesn't push me into telling him what happened at Carmen's. No flowers to try to cheer me up. No sappy text messages to check up on me. He's just here. He came to see if I was alright, even after I told him I didn't need anyone.

But I do need him. I need someone to tell me everything is going to be alright, even though I know it's not.

I pull away. "I'm so sorry about yelling at you. You probably think I'm the worst person ever." I wipe tears away, but they keep coming.

"No. I was beginning to worry you were too perfect. You have real emotions like a real human. It's good to let it all out." He gestures to the room. "Mind if I come join you for a while? I don't want you to be alone anymore."

All I can do is nod before bursting into tears.

♫

I expected Jax to leave me a long time ago. I've heard that guys aren't sure what to do when a girl cries, and I'm sure chasing down a furious, sobbing girl on the streets of Queens brought more attention to him than he would have liked. From Jax and the cabby, and the people standing around on the street that witnessed my breakdown . . .

It wasn't pretty.

Yet, here he sits on the bright red couch in his fancy hotel room he let me stay in, his arm around my shoulders as I cry into his soaking wet shirt.

I don't know how long it's been and I don't care. All the emotions that I've kept bottled up for the last however many years are finally coming out. And I can't seem to get a hold of myself and stop them.

Why do we have to cry when we're sad? It's the one thing I can't wrap my head around. And where does sadness even come from? Why does it have to be so extreme? So consuming? Because the emotions I'm experiencing right now feel like they're going to swallow me up and never let me go. Maybe that's why we cry. To let all the emptiness and pain out through our tears so we have room to bottle up new feelings and emotions until they're ready to break again.

I don't know. The truth is, I hate it.

For some reason, though, it does feel good to let everything out. I haven't cried in forever. Not like this. I can't remember the last time I cried like this. When did everything in my life became too much for me to handle? How did I come to feel so . . . helpless?

I expected the weirdness from Carmen. After all, abandoned children don't just show up on their wannabe super model parent's doorsteps every day. But what I didn't expect was to feel so empty. Carmen basically shunned me. What's stupid is I *should* have expected it. She did leave us, after all. And Dad warned me multiple times that she wouldn't care. But I expected a little more . . . empathy? More feelings? A hug? A pat on the back? Anything! But no. She's exactly the woman Dad said she was. She doesn't care.

And part of me is happy I know that now. I can at least have some closure on the whole thing. And I'm so glad Maddy wasn't here with me. She wouldn't have handled it as well as I did. As if me sobbing hysterically for hours on end is handling it well.

Maybe I'll feel better if I yell at someone. Or punch something. But I don't. Instead, I cuddle against Jax, listen as he books me a flight home, wipe my sore, puffy eyes with my bare, now wet arm, and let out a slow breath. "Okay. I think . . . I'm done."

He doesn't respond, just pulls me tighter against his shoulder.

"Sorry you had to see that. I think I've only had one meltdown in my entire life, and unfortunately you were here for it."

"Well, someone has to see you at your worst, right?"

I rub my puffy eyes, smearing mascara on my hand. "Yeah. Too bad I can't see you at yours."

"Trust me. You don't want to see it."

I ignore that. "I feel horrible I ruined the rest of your day being an emotional wreck. You can tell me 'I told you so' if you want. I know I'm gonna hear it from my dad right when I get home." I think about the flight home Jax booked for me for tomorrow morning. A part of me doesn't want to go. I don't know if I'm brave enough to face my family. They'll be so disappointed.

And facing Maddy? I can't even think about it right now.

"You had no idea what she was going to say. And neither did he. Don't feel bad about this. You tried. It's more than she's done her entire life. You should feel good that you actually put yourself out there and asked."

"She's not going to help, though. My sister . . ." I trail off and take a slow breath. "I get to go home now and she'll just keep getting worse. I don't know what else I can do."

"If I could help your sister, I would."

"I know." I wonder if he's a match. There's no way I'd ask him, though. Even if I feel like I know him better than

I know Carmen. It's not the right thing to do. Asking a stranger for a kidney? No way. There's no way.

He shifts in his seat and clears his throat. "Can I tell you something?"

"Sure. I'm pretty sure I've spilled all of my secrets to you today."

"Well, I'm about to spill the biggest one I have. I've never told anyone this. Not even my parents."

A million things run through my mind. What could this secret be? It sounds serious and part of me wants to tell him to keep it to himself, but the way he looks at me puts me at a loss for words. "Okay . . ."

"Don't worry. I'm not a serial killer or anything."

"That's a relief. You're not some crazy stalker or drug dealer or mob boss, are you?"

He chuckles, easing the tension from the room. "Not quite."

"Good. But for real. You kind of scared me there for a minute."

"Sorry." He grins and then his face falls and he's serious again. "So . . . my secret."

"You don't have to tell me if you don't want to."

"No, that's just it. I need to tell someone. I need to get it out. I want you to know. You've basically bared your soul to me today and I want you to know at least a little more about me." He swallows. "I'm not perfect. But I'm not a bad guy. The tabloids spread rumors and lies, but at times, some of those rumors can touch the truth a little." He sighs. "Last year when my dad died, I . . . kind of lost it.

I was on tour with my band, I wasn't with my family very often, I was fighting with my friends and hating performing every night with them. I didn't know how to deal. The pain of losing my dad was so . . . raw, you know?"

I nod. I don't know the feeling of losing someone like that, but I do know the feeling of knowing my sister's life hangs in the balance. And I can only imagine what will happen to me if I lose her.

"Anyway. I needed a way out. I was depressed. At first I went to a psychologist and talked about my problems. Which helped a little, but being on tour so much kind of makes things difficult sometimes. After that, I drank a lot. Drinking dulls the pain. It makes you not feel. And that was just what I needed. But it wasn't enough. So . . . I started taking prescription drugs. They were easy to find. All I had to do was ask around a bit. You'd never believe how many people have them. A lot of the roadies that travel with us have them. The rest of my band. It's like a part of the life, I guess. Hollywood life. You've seen how many famous people overdose. It's like candy there."

I stare at him. "What happened?"

"I snapped myself out of my screwed up life and realized I wasn't living the dream. I wasn't happy. I pushed everyone I loved away because all I was thinking of was the next time I could dull the pain."

"Your addiction was pretty bad then."

"Yeah."

"I'm sorry."

"Don't be. We all have choices. I just learned way too late that I made the wrong ones."

"But you're here. Now. Clean. At least I think?"

"I'm clean, yes, but it took a few months to get back to normal. As normal as life in Hollywood can get at least. I just wanted you to know that. My past isn't pretty. And if we were to ever . . . I don't know. Move forward in the future . . . I want you to know what you'd be getting yourself into."

"You seem like you're doing okay, from what you've already been through. How is your family doing with it all?"

"For a while I thought my family had given up on me. But I was so wrong. One day, when I was at a really low point, my mom called me and told me to come home. And I listened. Now before then, I didn't listen at all, so that was weird that I actually took her advice and acted. When I made the decision to get help, she checked me into a rehab facility. I was at my lowest of lows. It was the worst time in my entire life and honestly, I thought about suicide. I don't know if you've ever had a moment that was so dark you were convinced that light couldn't possibly find a way to slip through again?"

I shake my head. "I've never felt that way. I've had horrible days and weeks. The past year has been rough with Maddy, but I've never been so full of despair and in so much pain that I wanted it to end. Not like that anyway. Life is . . ." I pause, thinking of the right word, but decide to go with the obvious. "Life is hard. Really hard. But it's good and beautiful, with so many opportunities for happiness. The hard times suck, yeah, but the happiness and those little moments that make living worth it, that's why I've never had those thoughts. I like being me. I like being here. Pain and all."

He smiled. "I get that now. I have so much I still want to do. If I can just help one person realize their worth . . ."

"You could, you know."

"I know. I swear you have your life all figured out."

"Ha!" I don't mean to laugh, but he has no idea. "Did you not see me the last two hours? I've been a basket case up in here."

"Of course you have. Anyone would have if they had been in your situation. To be honest, I thought you handled it very well. Better than I would have. I don't blame you for freaking out. But I'm talking about before all that happened. The reason you came to New York in the first place. Even though you knew your mom left you when you were young, you weren't afraid to search her out and find her. You're so brave. You need to write this story down. True and hard stories are the most powerful ones out there."

"I don't write, but maybe you could do that for me, since you write lyrics and all." I smile. "As for coming to New York . . . I'll admit I was terrified. Not just because of a big unknown city, but tracking someone down who didn't want to be found was hard and really scary."

"Yes, but you still did it. You still had the courage to do it. Just like you had the courage to jump on that plane. The courage to trust a guy you barely met."

"Yeah, that was unexpected for sure. But I'm not that courageous. Trust me. And while I don't regret coming here, I do regret having as much hope as I did. You put your faith in your family. Family is everything. But when your family doesn't bat an eye when you ask for help? I don't know what to think anymore."

"Not all families are like that. Look at your dad. He would do anything for you and your siblings."

"I know. I just don't get it. I guess some people can just choose to forget their pasts completely. A coping mechanism? Because I will never, ever do what she did. Never." My voice echoes through the hotel room and I grimace.

"I know you won't."

"Sorry. Got carried away there."

"Don't say sorry." He's quiet for a moment as he grabs my hand. "So, what are you going to do now that you're going back home?"

"I haven't really thought about it."

"Of course you have."

I pause. "Well, I'll spend most of the time with Maddy. Do everything I can for her. I was thinking about donating one of my kidneys to someone else. Maybe work to audition for a piano scholarship for next year, since I definitely want to go to college once I graduate next spring. That much I know."

He's shaking his head, a smile on his face. "See? You've got it all figured out. If one thing doesn't work out, you'll do something else. Me? I have no idea what I want. Where I'll be."

"What do you want?"

He hesitates, and when he speaks, it's almost a whisper. "I want to be myself again. I want to make my own music. Not what someone tells me will sell. Just music that I love. And I want to stay clean."

"And what do you have to do to get there?"

"I don't know. Well, that's not true. I know how to stay clean, but I don't know what to do about my band. Or my contracts, manager, agent. There are so many things on the business side that are really tricky to figure out."

I think about that for a second and lay my head on his shoulder. "But you love music."

"Yes."

"You just don't like the spotlight?"

"You know, it isn't the spotlight that I don't like. I love performing. Performing live gives me a rush that nothing can compare to. It's the baggage that comes with it. Being gone for months on a tour and living out of a suitcase. Never seeing my family. The depression that comes with not having a normal life, which leads to things that squash that down. The crazy fans that recognize me everywhere I go. The stalkers. The paparazzi. It's just too much. If I could be behind the scenes, writing music and performing every once in a while, I'd do that."

"Do it then."

"I don't think I can."

"Why not?"

"It's . . . complicated. That's the only word that fits."

"There's nothing complicated about it. You want to take a different path in your life, do it."

He stands. "It's not that easy."

"But it is."

"No, it's not." He closes his eyes, his body tense. He lets out a long breath. "It means turning my back on my band, my manager, agent. I can't let so many people down."

"But look at you. Look at why you're even sitting here with me. Why you're in New York in the first place. You're miserable."

He doesn't answer and I don't push him. I can see I've struck a nerve. He shakes his head. "I'm sorry. It's just . . . hard. This life, it's not all it's cracked up to be."

"I've noticed." I give him a smile. "You'll get through it, though. You're strong. You know what you want. You just have to take that leap to get it."

He sits again and squeezes my shoulder. "I don't know what I'm going to do when you leave." He's quiet for a moment. "I've never had someone, besides my family, tell me to do what I want. You make it sound so easy."

"It could be easy. You just have to find a way around the fine print."

He smiles. "That's a great way of putting it."

"Thanks for calling the airport by the way. There's no way they could have understood me when I was freaking out."

He nods, not saying anything else, but yawns instead.

"You look tired."

"I am. Didn't sleep much last night."

"Do you need me to take you home?"

He laughs. "That would be a no. You'd never make it out alive driving in New York. And I just use cabs. Or I can call my sister if I really need to. But cabs, I'm afraid, are safer than riding with her."

"You're right." But I'm still worried about him. "You can stay here for a while. If you need to take a nap, go ahead."

"I don't want you to be uncomfortable."

"Look. You've seen me at my worst. I'm not uncomfortable and I don't think you're going to take advantage of me in any way. You're a gentleman. More so than the guys that go to my high school."

"My mom taught me right. And she would be proud to hear you say that."

"I like her already. Why don't you lie down for a little bit." I move out of the way and kneel on the floor so he can get comfortable. He lays back so his head is resting on the armrest and stretches his legs out until his feet are hanging off the other end of the couch. "So . . . have I mentioned you're pretty tall? Believe me, I noticed earlier, and you probably already know this, but you look like a giant on this couch with your legs hanging off."

"Thanks. I think."

He shoots me a smile that could seriously kill. And I realize he looks really good right now. Like . . . I want to make out with him good. But I'm not going to. I clear my throat to get my mind off things. "I'll get you a blanket or something." I start to stand, but he grabs my hand.

"I promise I'm not going to fall asleep."

"You can if you need to."

"Nah. This is nice to just relax for a bit."

I sit down on the floor, my hand in his. I lean my shoulder against the couch and then we're kind of looking right at each other. He reaches out, runs his fingers through a strand of my dark, probably super messy hair. "Your hair looks amazing when it's down."

"Oh?"

He kind of gets an embarrassed look on his face. "Yeah."

"Thank you."

He nods. "Are you dating anyone back home?"

The question kind of flies out of nowhere and catches me off guard. Of course I'm not dating anyone. I don't have time to date people. I swallow the guilt of hanging out with Jax. Of having feelings for him. I shouldn't be feeling this way while Maddy . . .

"No." My voice is smaller than I'd like, but I can't really do anything about that when he's looking at me the way he is.

"Why not?"

I shrug. "No one asks anyone out anymore. People just 'hang out.' Boys are dumb."

He laughs. "Yes. Yes we are."

"No offense to you, of course."

"Right." He squeezes my hand. "I dated a girl for a while. Two years, I think."

"Melanie Price?" I think of the singer that the paparazzi guy mentioned earlier today. A hot blond babe who always seemed to be busting out of her shirt. At least in the pictures I've seen of her.

He snorts. "That would be a no. This girl and I dated in high school. Freshman to junior year."

"Oh." This surprises me. "What happened?"

"I moved to L.A. And she moved on."

"Oh. That's . . . sad."

"It's fine. She's happy as far as I know. Married with a kid, I think. She got married right after high school."

I think about what it would be like to have a relationship with someone famous. I'm sure it wouldn't work out. "I've always seen Hollywood guys dating Hollywood girls anyway though. It makes sense if you think about it. The singers and the actors. You know. There's a million stories like that."

He rolls his eyes. "I don't date girls from Hollywood. Besides Tessa White, but that was like two weeks. We were really just friends, that's pretty much it. But someone always has to turn it into something else. The only reason we ended up going out a few times was because our publicists wanted us to have a story in the news for a while. To shake things up or whatever. You know, hardcore rocker falls for small-town country singer."

"Sounds . . . Awesome? Was it all you ever dreamed it would be and more?"

He wrinkles his nose. "Not really. I hate country."

"Well, considering you're a rock kind of guy, that doesn't surprise me at all."

All he does is smile. He turns on his side and shivers.

He's so close. So close I can feel his breath on my cheek. I want him to kiss me. It's the only thing running through my cloudy head now.

Jax's phone rings and he lets out some colorful words before checking to see who it is. "Sorry," he says. "Sometimes I don't think before I talk." He glances at his phone and smiles before he sits up and answers. "Hey, Jeigh."

I try to find something to keep me busy so I don't listen to his conversation, but there's nothing for me to do but sit here.

He stands and walks over to the window while he listens to whatever she's saying. "Yeah. Okay." Pause. "No." Pause. "I just haven't." Pause. "Really?" He laughs. "That's fine." Pause. "No, I'm at the hotel." He smiles at me. "Yes, with that girl. Her name's Mia, by the way." The smile is wider now. "I'll tell you later." He winks at me. "Okay. See you soon." He hangs up. "Jeigh is in the area and invited us to dinner if you want to come with me."

"Me?"

He looks around. "No one else is here."

"True." I pull myself up on the couch as he plops down next to me. "Aren't you too tired?"

"I'm fine."

"Okay."

"Okay you'll come?"

I shrug. "Sure." It will definitely help cheer me up. And I don't leave to go home until tomorrow anyway. Might as well do something fun on my last night in New York. Because I'll probably never ever come back here again.

"I'll call her real quick. Be right back." He goes in the other room. I hear the bathroom door shut after he hangs up with her.

A few minutes later, I look up as he comes back in, hair looking better, his eyes not as tired as before. To be honest, I could stare at him all night. "You look great."

"I look the same as I did earlier." He grins.

Heat flushes my face. "Right."

He sits down, puts his arm around my shoulders, and surprises me as he kisses me on the cheek. "Thank you. For everything."

I'll never wash my cheek again.

CHAPTER 23

I'll take your hand and you'll take mine,
We'll leave our troubles far behind
I'd love to get away from here
Run away from my life, to be with you my dear.
—J.S.

The air is warm, the lights bright as we stroll down the sidewalk toward Times Square. It takes him a few minutes, but Jax finally reaches out and takes my hand, which makes me feel all giddy inside. And not because he's famous.

It's because I kind of like him. Okay, I like him. He's kind and selfless and so real. Which is the total opposite of any movie star or rockstar I've ever read about. I guess there are some nice ones out there, but you never know what they're really like from all the shows on TV and videos on the Internet. And Jax? I feel like he's been real with me for the short time I've been with him. I've seen a side of him I'm not sure he's shown a lot of people. Like he said, no one really knows the real him. They know the rumors and the stories that make him popular, but not *him*.

But I feel like I do.

My heart skips a beat when I realize something: I'm leaving tomorrow and will probably never see him again.

I don't know how I feel about that. But then I think of Maddy and the guilt creeps in. How can I sit here and enjoy myself when Carmen destroyed any hope I had left for saving her? How can I fall for someone when Maddy will now never get that chance?

It's a lot to take in. I came to New York full of hope, and tomorrow I'll leave with nothing but sorrow and guilt and disappointment.

"Watch out," Jax says as he pulls me around a pile of bags on the sidewalk. I snap back to attention and leave my thoughts of despair behind for the moment.

There are several things I never knew before coming to this city. One, businesses in New York set their garbage on the sidewalk next to the curb every night so the garbage trucks can come pick it up the next morning. And some of those piles of garbage are taller than I am and obviously do not smell good when we walk by. They've been sitting in the heat, fermenting for hours, leaking onto the street. But it's garbage, I guess. It's not supposed to smell like scented candles or flowers. Still, it's kind of weird. Where I come from, we have garbage cans we set out once a week. And rarely does my town—even the downtown—ever have *this* much garbage. Kind of takes the shine off the big city, in a way.

Two. So many people walk here. Like, almost everyone. There aren't a lot of cars. Well, I guess I should rephrase that. There are tons of vehicles, but most are taxis. And they're everywhere. People either walk, taxi, or take the subway since the traffic is a nightmare. Plus, I've seen the prices posted on the garages. Hundreds of dollars just to park every month? No, thanks. I know I'd never own a car if I lived here.

Ha. Me living in a big city like this? Not likely. I like the calm. And it's so busy here. There's noise all the time. Every hour of the day and night. Honking cars, people yelling things out their car windows and at each other on the sidewalks, sirens, music blasting from car stereos or from bands playing on the street, and fun stuff like that.

And then there are the buildings. They're enormous. As we walk down the street, all I can see when I look up are buildings. Brick and glass, so many stories up. I'm feeling claustrophobic again, so I tighten my grip on Jax's hand and move closer to him. Which doesn't make sense when you're claustrophobic, but hey, it works for me.

He must notice my uneasiness. "You okay?"

"Yeah."

"We're almost there." He picks up our pace and we pass crowds of people as the lights get brighter. He's still wearing his hat, avoiding eyes and keeping to himself. I don't blame him.

And then we're standing in Times Square, surrounded by crowds and crowds of people. And it's fabulous. And so beautiful to the point it's overwhelming. There is so much to take in. Pictures and movies don't do it justice. Like at all. I never ever thought I'd ever stand here. But here I am.

"Wow." It's the only word that comes to my mouth. "Can you . . . uh . . . can we take a picture? I mean, I don't have to take one with you if you don't want to, but—."

"Of course." He pulls out his phone and I pull out mine. "I'm not a fan of selfies, but if you're in the picture with me, I'll be happy to take one."

"Yeah, I'm kind of anti-selfie, myself. But like you said. We'll both be in it. We should call it a double selfie."

He laughs. "Sounds about right."

I step beside him and he wraps one arm around me as he holds his phone up to snap the picture. I hopefully give it my best smile. Which usually doesn't happen. I'm not the most photogenic person in the world and I'm not ashamed to admit it. "Here. Can you do mine, too?"

He takes my phone and we both smile again. "Hopefully I don't look too stupid," he says. He hands it back to me and I'm shaking my head.

"That's not possible." I pull up the picture and smile. I really want to text it to Maddy, but I'd rather talk to her in person. At least about this. And she's so sick. The last thing I want to do is make it seem like I'm at my happiest and off on a vacation when she's at her worst and stuck in the hospital.

I miss her. I need to see her and make sure she's okay. Because she's not okay. She'll never be okay.

The emotions from the conversation with Carmen come back full force then and I struggle to keep them under control. I can cry later. When I'm alone.

Jax leans over my shoulder then to look at the picture. "We look good together."

I nod, but then stop, realizing what he said. I look at him out of the corner of my eye and blush under his gaze. The intensity of that gaze almost knocks me down. After I catch my breath, he takes my hand again.

"You ready?"

"Yeah." It's all I can say. I can't get over the way he looked at me. No one's ever looked at me like that before.

And that's when I realize I need to get out of here. I need to be home with Maddy. Not that I've forgotten her at all, but I shouldn't be here. Not now. Not when she's waiting for me with no idea what has happened with Carmen. She still has that hope. The hope I lost the second I walked out Carmen's door.

"Jax," I say as we walk toward the restaurant. "I want to go back to the hotel. I . . . need to get ready to go tomorrow." Not that I have a lot to pack. Just the crap I shoved in my backpack.

"You're not hungry?"

"Well, yeah, but, I just . . ." I don't know how to explain what I'm feeling to him, but he nods anyway.

"I'll order you some room service then."

"You're not mad?"

He shakes his head. "Of course not. You've had a hard day."

I nod, not able to speak for the wave of emotions welling up again. It *has* been a long day. And I need to get out of this fantasy and get back to my real life with my sister.

She needs me.

We turn around and start our walk back to the hotel.

"I wish you could stay," Jax says, his baseball cap low over his eyes.

"I have to get home for Maddy. And . . . I'm not meant for the city."

He lets out a long sigh. "Neither am I."

There are a lot of people on the streets and I hang on tight as he pulls me through the crowd. Once we're kind of to ourselves, I speak again. "You know how to handle the big city, though. I'd get lost in the madness and never be able to find myself again."

He plays with his eyebrow ring a moment, then puts his hand down. "You just have to remember who you are." I smile as he reaches out and runs his knuckles down my cheek. "You wouldn't forget yourself. You're too strong."

I snort. Which is the worst possible thing I could do at the moment, but oh well. The moment deserved a snort. "I'm only strong when I have to be."

"I know." He stares straight ahead and messes with his eyebrow ring again.

I have to say, even though I'm still not a huge fan of piercings, it's kind of growing on me.

We reach the hotel and Jax walks me to my room again. "You can find your way from here?" he asks when the elevator door opens on my floor. He puts the password in and swipes his keycard.

I chuckle. "Yeah, I think so." I fold my arms, ignoring the beating of my heart and the feelings of . . . I don't know what . . . That come rushing through my body.

I like him.

I can't.

But what if I could?

I can't.

"I'm sorry about tonight," I say.

"It's no big deal. Jeigh will understand."

"She was so nice. Tell her good-bye for me, okay?"

"I will."

I reach out and take his hand. "Thank you. For everything."

He stares at our hands and pulls me to him, wrapping his strong arms around me. "I'll pick you up tomorrow morning and ride with you to the airport." he says, resting his chin on the top of my head. "If that's okay?"

"More than okay." As I pull away and head into my room, I'm confused. I really do like him. And I really, really want him to kiss me. Like really. But he can't. There's no point. So many cant's and not enough can's.

It's all for the best, though. I'm leaving tomorrow. I'll probably never see him again. Why would we start something we can't finish? I don't want to be a fling. I want more than that. I want something real.

"Don't forget to order yourself some dinner. It's on me," he says.

"Okay."

"Bye."

"Bye." I see him put his hand up to wave good-bye as I close the door.

Sometimes love stories suck.

CHAPTER 24

The only phrase that describes what I feel doesn't do it justice.
The words come out, but here I sit, miserable and alone.
I miss you
—J.S.

Jax sits next to me at the airport, one hand in mine and one resting on his knee. We watch people in silence as they go from here to there, rushing, meandering, happy, sad. The rush of emotions I feel is overwhelming to say the least. I can't describe them, so I'm quiet. Calm. Worried about Maddy. Not ready to leave Jax.

"So, are you glad you came? Or do you regret it?" he asks.

"I don't regret coming here. I do regret the hope I had before I came, though. I thought it would be a simple task and it turned out to be nothing at all. I wish I could have done more for Maddy. Something. I just . . . don't know what else I could have done."

He nods. "If it makes you feel any better, I'm glad you came."

"Me too. Even if we had the weirdest meet-cute, ever."

"Meet-cute?"

"When a guy and a girl meet the first time. If you remember right, I insulted you and your band. Pretty bad."

"Best. Meet-Cute. Ever."

"If you say so," I say, chuckling.

As we sit there together, knowing the inevitable is coming, I feel a sense of loss, I think. I admit the feelings I have for Jax are new. Fresh. Ridiculous after only a few days of meeting each other.

But they're real. Intense. Raw. I grieve for him already and we haven't even said good-bye yet. I grieve for the memories we've made, the things we've shared. His past addictions and life full of the spotlight and lies.

I wish I could ask him to come with me, but I know it won't happen. We have very different lives. Different struggles we're both dealing with. We need to figure things out independently before anything could ever happen between us. The timing is off.

Such is my life.

My eyes fall on our entwined hands. I never expected to have a whirlwind romance while trying to save my sister's life. It feels so wrong. But I couldn't have finished this journey without Jax. In so many ways, he helped me do what needed to be done. And I'll never be able to repay him for that.

I know it's insane to think, but he's perfect for me. I know it, and even though I don't know if he knows it, I'm sure he feels something. He has to. But we both know we can't be together. It would never work. The small-town girl and the Hollywood rockstar only works in the movies. And this is real life.

Real life, where I'll go home to watch my sister die with only my parents to comfort me. Everyone else I know will walk around on eggshells before and after it happens and they'll ask if there's anything they can do for me, and I'll reply no.

I still cling to the slight hope that she'll move to the top of the donor list, but I know it's a long shot. I'm going to have to prepare myself if things get worse. I have to prepare myself to let her go.

I wish real life was more like fairytales sometimes. It would be much easier to deal with an evil queen than a nasty disease. Sure, they're both scary and death is usually involved, but in the fairytales, everything works out for the best. The princess is inches from death and the prince always finds a way to save her or she finds a way to save herself.

It's probably almost time for me to head upstairs to my gate. I wish Jax could come with me, but I know they won't let him through security, despite his celebrity status.

I pull out my phone and look at the time. "I'd better get going. I have to go through security and stuff to get to my gate."

He nods.

I stand and sling my purse over my shoulder while I pick up my backpack. I don't know what to say, so I just look at him and smile.

"I wish we had more time," he says.

"Me too."

"I've only known you a few days, but I swear I've

known you forever. I don't . . ." He clears his throat. "I don't want to . . ."

"Say good-bye?" I finish for him.

He nods. "Yeah."

"Good-byes are never easy." I lean forward and wrap my arms around his waist, leaning my head against his chest and breathing in the scent of him, perhaps for one last time. We live a whole gigantic country away. And long-distance relationships never last. Or so I've heard. "Thank you. For everything."

I feel his chin on the top of my head as he pulls me close. "No. Thank you, Mia. I hope everything works out for your sister. You both deserve to be happy."

"Thanks." I don't know what else to say. I'm positive this is the last time I'll ever see him. Besides on TV and videos online, I guess. If he wanted to, he could forget me in a few days, seeing how more than half the country's women are in love with him. He has a crazy lifestyle and mine's just boring in comparison. But I'd rather my boring over his crazy, I think.

I know I'll never forget him, though. He took a chance on a stranger. Even after that stranger insulted him and his band the first time he met her. I'll treasure the memories I've made with him. "Well . . . good-bye." I let my hands slide from his and turn to walk away.

I almost make it to the escalator to go upstairs when someone grabs my arms and whirls me around. "What the—"

Jax leans in close, his blue eyes searching mine. "Do you believe in fate, Mia?"

"I . . ."

"Because I can't help but feel like we were meant to meet. I know that sounds super cheesy, but it's true."

"Fate. Honestly, I have a hard time with fate. I don't trust it. It's fickle and indecisive. Just when you think fate has lent you a helping hand, it rips that hand away and puts disappointment in its place."

"I agree. To a point. But I've never . . . You . . ." He struggles to find the right words. "You have no idea how much meeting you has changed my perspective. On a lot of things, actually. My band, my problems. My life. I don't think I can handle seeing you walk away from me forever. I just found you." He touches my face, his knuckles skimming my cheekbone. "I don't want to lose you. Not now."

"Jax, I . . ." I trail off. I know I'm out of time. If I don't get to my gate, I'll miss my flight. And every extra second I spend here is one I don't get to spend with Maddy. But there's so much I want to tell him, and I can't find the words. So I do the only thing I can think that will show him how I'm feeling.

I kiss him.

He reacts by wrapping his arms around my waist and pulling me close. I melt into him and savor the moment as long as I can. The kiss is kind of intense for prying eyes, but for once, I don't care. It's everything a first and last kiss should be. Full of passion, regrets, screwed up emotions, and a bit of sorrow. Perfect.

I finally pull back, just a little, still not believing I kissed him first, but mentally applauding the spontaneity of it.

"Please, take care of yourself." I meet his gaze, his blue eyes beautiful, glistening with what look like tears.

"I will." He leans his forehead against mine and sighs. "Have a safe flight. Is it . . . okay if I call you? Maybe I can come visit sometime? You know, if you don't mind. I have some things to do, of course, like figure out my career and stuff, but . . . in the future?"

"Of course I wouldn't mind." I smile, but the rational part of my brain doesn't believe that will ever happen. Out of all the girls in the world, why would he fly across the country to visit me? I'm a nobody compared to everyone else he knows.

He clears his throat. I know he's just as affected from the kiss as I am. "Oh, and take this so you're not bored." He pulls his MP3 player and some earbuds out of his pocket and sets them in my hand.

"I can't take these. They're yours."

He closes my hand around them and smiles. "I can afford another." He winks. "And besides, I want you to have something to remember me by. Until I . . . figure things out."

Emotion bubbles way too close to the surface and all I can do is nod as I swallow the lump in my throat. "Thank you. Good luck with whatever you have to do. I know you're brave enough to do it."

He leans forward, kissing my forehead, and backs away as I turn to go up the escalator. For real this time. My foot hits the step and I start to rise, but I turn around and keep my eyes on him as I move farther away. He stands in the same place, his hands in his pockets, wearing his same old hat, a sad smile on his face.

I squeeze the MP3 player in my hand, thankful for a small part of him to take with me. Before I turn the corner, I take one last look at him and lift my hand in a small wave. He waves back, and I swear to myself I won't cry.

CHAPTER 25

Can you fall in love with a single glance?
Is it madness to think there could be a chance?
When I gaze in your eyes, it has to be true.
I fell hard the moment I looked at you.
—J.S.

The plane ride home is boring. I spend half the time listening to Jax's music, even though I swore I'd never like his stuff.

But as I listen to the lyrics, I realize how much of himself he puts in his music. How many demons he's fighting. How unhappy he is. It makes me want to run back into his arms and save him.

But I have someone else to save.

Dad's waiting in the terminal as I ride down the escalator. He doesn't say a word, just hugs me tight when I step off.

"Thanks for coming to meet me. Did Mom drop you off?"

He nods. "We'll take your car home together since you left it here. I just . . . didn't want you to drive home alone."

I smile at that. He always worries about me. Always. "How's Maddy?"

He shrugs. "I'd rather talk to you in the car. Why don't we grab your suitcases and we'll go straight to the hospital."

"This is all I have." I turn so he can see my backpack on my shoulder.

He raises an eyebrow. "You took one bag to New York? You?"

I shrug. "I was in a hurry."

"That you were." He takes my backpack from me and I follow him to the car. "I never thought I'd see the day."

"Honestly, me either."

"Where'd you get the new earbuds?"

I shrug. "A friend from school let me borrow them."

"Huh."

Dad's quiet on the way home. We talk briefly about the weather in New York versus California. How the plane ride home was. What Zack has been building with his Legos. He doesn't ask how my visit went. Since Carmen didn't accompany me home and I didn't call with good news, I'm sure he knows that it did not go well. I'm kind of grateful he doesn't ask me about it. I don't think I can handle it right now.

"So . . . is Maddy okay? You never answered me."

He takes a long, deep breath and rubs a hand over his face. "I wanted to wait until we got to the hospital, but I guess now is as good a time as any." He glances over at me, his grip tight on the steering wheel. "She's not doing well, honey. Even the doctors are losing hope. She's been moved up on the waiting list, but I'm not convinced we'll find a donor in time." He sniffs and wipes at his eyes. "Sorry."

"It's okay, Dad." I reach over and put my hand on his arm, giving it a squeeze and trying to keep my own emotions in check.

"I just feel like I failed her. I've done everything to keep your sister alive, but I feel like I haven't done anything at the same time. It should be me. She's too young to . . . I don't know how I'll handle it if . . ."

He shakes his head and swallows, not saying anything else. He doesn't have to. We both know what could happen soon enough.

♫

Twenty minutes later, after driving the rest of the way in silence, I'm sitting next to Maddy's hospital bed, listening to the sound of the annoying machines beeping all around us.

If they weren't connected to her, I'd unplug them if I could.

It's hard to look at her. She looks like a ghost of her old self. I wasn't prepared for this. For how different she'd be in only three days.

I shouldn't have left. My trip was worthless. I squeeze Jax's MP3 player in my hand. Maybe it wasn't totally worthless, even though I didn't get what I went for. And I really don't want to admit Dad was right. To anyone.

She stirs, turning her face toward me as she opens her eyes. "Mia?"

"Hey, Maddy. How are you feeling?"

She tries to laugh but only a cough comes out. "Been better. Much better." She reaches for my hand and I take hers. It's cold. "I'm glad you're back. I missed you."

"Believe me. I missed you, too."

"Did Mom pick you up?"

"Dad. And I swear I got the first flight back here that I could. It took a while. I'm sorry."

She shakes her head. "I'm sorry I cut your trip short."

"It wasn't a trip, Maddy. The only reason I went was for you."

"I know. But if my stupid body would function the way it was supposed to, neither of us would be sitting here right now." She grimaces as she moves and shivers. "Could you grab that blanket and pull it over my knees for me?"

I do as she says and make sure she's tucked in good enough. She thanks me and adjusts the oxygen buds in her nose. "How was New York then?"

I can't look her in the eye, so all I do is shrug and stare at the IV in her frail hand.

"That good, huh?"

"Yeah."

She stares at the IV drip, too, watches it for a while. "What was she like?"

I've rehearsed this conversation over and over in my head ever since I got on the plane this morning and I still don't know what to say to her. So, instead of sugarcoating it, I go with the truth. "She's . . . just like Dad said she was. She doesn't care."

She closes her eyes and takes a shaky breath. She takes a moment, and when she opens them, I can see tears welling. "Was she nice? Did she ask about me? Did she show any emotion when you told her? Any at all?"

"No. She was . . . cold. Distant. I don't know how Dad ever married someone like her."

"I've always pictured her that way."

"Really?" I wonder why she never told me this. We've talked about Carmen plenty of times, but she's never admitted that to me.

"Yeah. Weird, huh? I just don't understand how a happy-go-lucky person could just up and abandon her kids like that. She has to be . . . messed up somehow. Or living with some type of issue." She touches the tape on the back of her hand and picks at the corner of it. "It's pretty awful. What she did. I forgive her, of course, but it's just . . ." She blinks, trying not to cry again.

"I don't know if I can forgive her, Maddy. I thought I could, but now?"

"You can forgive her because she's not a part of our lives and you'll probably never see her again. It's easier to do when you think of it like that."

"Possibly." But I can't stop thinking about her. Her expressionless face, her voice. It's too fresh and raw. Maybe when time passes, I'll be able to forget it.

"Was it, you know, hard to stay in control of your emotions? I know you. You didn't freak out, did you?"

"What do you mean, you know me?" I ask.

She just smiles and shakes her head.

"Yeah, I know. Sometimes I can be a bit . . . much. And to answer your question, yes, I was able to control my emotions. For the most part. Though, I did freak out a little. Toward the end." I pause. "She has a daughter. Another one. She's thirteen and looks a lot like you."

Her eyes are wide as I'm sure mine were when I first saw her. "What's her name?"

"Clarissa."

"Does she treat her well?"

I shrug. "Looked like it. I was only there for maybe fifteen minutes, but from what I saw . . . she looked like she was loved."

She nods and folds her arms, probably thinking the news is just as weird as I think it is. "That's good, I guess. Good that she cares enough about someone at least. I'm sorry you had to face her alone." She yawns and moves around to get comfortable again.

"It's fine. I'm just glad you weren't there. You're too sweet to talk to someone like her. She wasn't rude, but she wasn't nice either. Like I said. Cold."

"I'm not that sweet."

"Whatever. You know you are."

She pulls her blankets up further and buries her arms underneath. "Sorry. It's super cold in here."

"You're fine." It's not cold at all. I think of how much weight she's lost and it's no wonder she's cold.

We sit in comfortable silence for a bit until she closes her eyes and freaks me out with how still she is. As I stare at her, my heart speeds up. "Maddy? You okay?"

She jumps and her eyes fly open. "Oh. Sorry."

"It's okay. You need to sleep."

She shakes her head. "Why does everyone keep saying that? I'm fine." She closes her eyes again and her deep breaths tell me she's asleep.

I sit next to her for a long time.

CHAPTER 26

I see the helplessness in your eyes.
The darker parts of yourself you hide.
Still you fight, you persevere.
To save a soul that you hold dear.
It will be all right, it will be okay.
Just keep hanging on for one more day.
—J.S.

Dad wakes me up a few hours later. I didn't even realize I'd fallen asleep. "Come on, sweetie. You've been here all night. Let me take you home."

"I want to stay with her." I glance at Maddy's sleeping form. She still looks so pale.

"She'll be fine for tonight. If anything changes, the doctor will call us and I'll bring you right back." He reaches out a hand to help me up. "I was just talking to the doctor a little bit ago. They ran a few more tests while you were gone to see if there's any other medication they can try. They have a new plan and we'll talk to them tomorrow about it."

"Will it make a difference?"

"You never know." It takes me a minute to let that sink

in and I let him help me up. "Bye, Maddy," I whisper and follow him out of the room.

Dad's quiet on the drive home. Again. He stares straight ahead, both hands on the steering wheel. He looks exhausted. "I'm glad you're home, honey."

"Me, too." And I am.

"Next time, which hopefully there's not a next time, please talk to me before you do something so rash. I was worried sick about you the entire time."

I smile. "Sorry you worried, but I was really fine. You're going to have to get used to letting me go anyway. I'm eighteen now, Dad."

He runs a hand through his hair. "I know. You could have asked me, though."

"There's no way you would have let me go if I would have asked."

"You're right. I wouldn't have." He's quiet for a moment as I stare out the window at the passing houses. "What did she say to you?" His voice is quieter. I can sense sadness behind his words, but his face doesn't show any emotion.

"She was just like you described. Not like us."

He nods, his Adam's apple bobbing as he swallows. "She wasn't mean to you, was she?"

I shrug. "Define *mean*?"

He sighs. "I'm so sorry, Mia. I tried to tell you."

"I know. I'm sorry I didn't listen. You were right, I was wrong. I'm not sorry I went, though. It was good for me to see her. To finally know what she's really like. You know? To put it all behind me and appreciate what I have."

"Yeah, I know."

I shift in my seat so I'm turned toward him. "I had a question. Why did you marry her at all? If she was so cold then, why were you attracted to someone like that?"

"She wasn't always that way." He frowns. "She changed. I don't even know what changed her."

"It was Maddy and me. She said it in a roundabout way. She didn't want us. We were too much for her to handle."

"She said that?"

"Not those exact words but pretty much."

"You know I love you, right?"

"Yeah, Dad. I know."

"You did nothing wrong, honey. I promise. You were a beautiful, sweet, smart, amazing child. As was your sister. Carmen's selfishness made her leave. She didn't want any responsibilities. I did. I don't regret anything. I don't regret how things worked out. It's been an honor raising you both. A privilege. You're my girls." His voice chokes on the last word and he hurries and wipes his eyes. I reach over to grab his hand and give it a reassuring squeeze.

I've never seen Dad cry before tonight. First on the drive home from the airport, and now he's doing it again. And it affects me more than I can admit. But I keep it together and try to be strong and let him be the vulnerable one for once.

"I wouldn't change anything either. Thank you for raising me. For being there for me even when I do stupid things."

"I love you girls. I don't want to see you hurt. Especially by Carmen. I'm sorry. For everything."

"Don't be sorry. You're the best dad I could ever ask for."

"Thanks, honey."

The rest of the drive is quiet, but it's a comfortable silence.

As we pull into the driveway, I see Mom's face in the window. She's outside before we go in the garage. When I'm out of the car, she hugs me so tight I lose my breath. She puts her hands on either side of my face, tears in her eyes. "Are you okay? I was so worried."

"I'm fine, Mom."

She wraps her arm around me and walks me inside. "Please don't ever do that again. Your dad almost had a heart attack when he found your note."

"Sorry."

She rests her head on mine as we walk. "I would have gone with you, you know. You just had to ask."

"I know." And I do know. Dad wouldn't have let me go, but Mom would have gone with me in a heartbeat.

She takes my bag from me. "I'm sure you're hungry. There are leftovers in the kitchen if you'd like some. Spaghetti. I made something normal because I knew you were coming home tonight."

"Thanks." My stomach growls, but I don't want to eat. I'm too tired to do anything. Thoughts of Maddy run through my head, along with thoughts of Jax. I just need to go to bed to clear all the emotions I have hanging around. I don't like feeling this way. All . . . Whiplashy. "I think I'm just going to go to bed though."

"You sure?"

"Yeah. I'm pretty tired."

"Okay." She rubs my back as I head to my room and I can feel her eyes on me even as I shut the door.

I throw my purse in the corner and glance around. My room looks the same. The same posters, the same quotes on my mirror. The yellow bedspread and matching curtains. My spotless floor.

And I just realized how boring I am. I need to spice something up in here. Change some colors. Maybe paint my walls. But not tonight. I'm ready to collapse I'm so tired.

With that thought, I get ready for bed.

I go through the motions. Brush teeth, bathroom, hair in ponytail, lamp on, light off, get in bed, lamp off. Before I go to sleep, I pull out my phone. As I click on pictures, the first one I see is the picture of me and Jax in New York. We look like a real couple. Like we've been together forever. We look comfortable. Safe.

It makes me miss him even more.

My phone flashes and I stare at the text message that just came in.

From him.

Jax: Thank you. For everything.

That's all it says.

It seems so final. Like a last good-bye. Like one of those movies where the couple has one amazing weekend together and never see each other again. The first one that comes to mind is *Serendipity*.

"Serendipity," I say. What a fun, yet interesting word. Maybe we'll be like that couple and not see each other for a while, but then find each other again. It's not like Jax even knows where the heck I live. All he has is my name and number. That's it.

I stare at it for a while longer, wondering what to do. I shouldn't leave his number in my phone. If I do, I'll just stare at it like an obsessed fan with nothing better to do, waiting for him to call. Text. Anything. And yet in my heart, I know it may never happen. Celebrities have flings all the time. I hope I wasn't a fling to him, but you never know.

I don't want to be one of those girls.

Instead of texting back, my finger hovers over my phone for a second before I gather enough courage to delete his number. It's not like I'll ever use it again anyway. And if I really need to get a hold of him, I can just look at my phone bill and find his number that way. They keep call and message records and crap like that every month. But it feels right to have it off my actual phone for some reason. Even though it hurts more than I thought it would.

I glance at our picture again before I lie on my pillow and let out a sigh as a tear slides down my cheek.

CHAPTER 27

Somewhere beneath the moon and stars, I hope you're thinking of me too.
—J.S.

It's been a week since New York and Maddy's not any better. In fact, she's getting worse. Instead of letting her come home, she's stuck in the hospital so the doctors can monitor her. She has her dialysis treatments there, is hooked up to an IV all the time, and gets bored as heck just sitting there. As I visit her each day, watching her fade a little bit more every time, I know I'm not going to be able to handle it when she decides to stop fighting.

There's nothing anyone can do but wait for a donor. And waiting for a donor means someone else has to die. Which is kind of a morbid and horrible thought. Wanting someone to die to save my sister. Wanting someone else to lose someone they love to save someone I love.

It's not fair.

But no one ever said life would be fair.

"Will you turn that TV down?" Mom asks as she walks into Maddy's room. "It's too late for it to be that loud." I frown and push the mute button.

"Happy now?"

Her eyes narrow. "I just don't want to wake up your sister."

"She can sleep through anything. She's always been like that." I watch as Mom smoothes Maddy's hair down and pats her hand before taking a seat next to the bed.

"How was she today?"

I shrug. "No change."

"Has she been awake at all?"

"Not really."

"Thanks for staying with her. I couldn't get off work today."

"Of course."

"Do you need anything?"

"No." I don't know why I'm in such a bad mood, but I am. "Thanks," I add. I don't want her to think I'm mad at her. I'm not. I'm just mad at the world in general.

Mom's phone rings. "It's Dad." She glances at Maddy. "Be right back." She hurries and steps outside as she answers her phone.

The room's silent, save for the ticking clock on the wall. "Mia?"

My eyes widen as Maddy whispers my name. I about jump off my chair and go to her. "Maddy? I'm here. You okay?"

She reaches out and takes my hand. Her face is white and her breathing labored. "It hurts."

Tears prick my eyes. "What does?"

"Everything."

I pull her blanket around her and try my best to make her more comfortable. "Do you need me to get the nurse?"

She slowly shakes her head. "I just . . . don't leave me. Okay?"

"Never." I keep hold of her hand and climb on the bed next to her. She leans her head on my shoulder and I feel hot tears soak through my shirt. My lip quivers. "You're crying."

"Am I?" She sniffs.

"I'm the emotional one. Not you." My eyes fill with tears. "Don't cry, Mads. Please don't cry."

"Can't help it." Her shoulders quake as I quietly rock her body. "I just . . . I'm going to miss you so much."

"Don't say that." Tears slide down my cheeks and lose themselves in her hair.

"I love you, Mia." Her grip tightens as much as it can and I squeeze back, making sure I don't hurt her. "I just . . . want you to . . . know that. I love you." Her entire body shakes in my arms as she cries.

I can feel a sob coming, but I hold it in long enough to tell her the same. "I love you, too."

CHAPTER 28

Safety lies with only you.
Before, I never knew what to do.
Who I was, or where I'd be.
I'm finding myself. Finding me.
                                    —*J.S.*

After spending all day yesterday at the hospital, my parents made me stay home today. And I feel the need to do something. Anything to keep my mind off Maddy. So here I sit at the piano, my fingers running over the slick, ivory keys. I don't know what to play today. Something sad? Something happy? I have no idea. The music isn't coming to me, so I just sit and stare. A melody does fill my senses, but instead of sharing it with everyone else, I decide to keep it locked away. A song that will never be heard by anyone but me.

Man, I'm depressing.

I plunk my fingers down on a chord and let them take over. When I realize what I'm playing, a Blue Fire song, I pull my fingers away and smack myself softly on the cheek for good measure

Stop it, Mia. Quit being an annoying love-sick girl. It's time to move on.

233

Move on from what, though? We didn't even have anything.

But I know we did. And that's what hurts the most.

Mom pokes her head into the music room. "Oh. You're in here? I thought you were outside."

"Nope." I've been sitting here for an hour at least. I don't know what's wrong with me. I've never had a hard time playing before.

"You okay?"

"Fine." I give her a super fake smile, but she doesn't notice.

"Oh. Good. Are you on dinner tonight?"

"I don't remember."

"Can you be? I'm going up to the hospital right now to sit with Maddy."

"Can I come?"

She shakes her head. "You need to relax here today. We know you haven't been sleeping well. Take a nap. Get some sleep tonight. You can come with me tomorrow."

"Fine."

"So . . . dinner?"

"Sure." I stand and walk slowly down the hall. "What does everyone want?"

"Whatever. Just something healthy. I'll see you guys later."

"Healthy shmealthy," I mutter under my breath as she shuts the garage door. I'm sure Mom will be in Heaven eating at the hospital tonight. I swear she secretly orders the unhealthy stuff when we're not there while we sit at home and eat . . . Tofu. And fat-free crap.

Nice.

Is it too much to ask for a nice, fat cheeseburger?

"What does everyone want for dinner? Dad? Zack?"

"Whatever," Dad yells.

"Pizza!" Zack shouts from downstairs.

I look through our pantry and cringe at the bareness of it. There's seriously nothing to eat. Kale chips? Really? I scowl at the bag and grab a little pack of Cheetos sitting next to it. They're probably Zack's, but I don't care tonight. I'll buy him another one. I don't know why he gets to eat yummy stuff, when Mom won't let the rest of us eat anything.

I plop down at the table, open the Cheetos, and finish the bag off in less than a minute, I swear. I even lick the cheese off my fingers. I feel satisfied.

The doorbell rings and I don't hear anyone running to get it so I sigh and stand. "Don't worry about getting up, guys. I'm on it." No one in this family ever answers the door but me. They do the same thing with the landline. If it rings, no one picks up the freaking phone. Drives me crazy. We even have caller ID. And if you don't know who's at the door, look out the window. Not that hard.

"Thanks!" Dad laughs from the other room and I smile. It's good to hear him laughing. We don't have a lot of laughter in the house these days.

I shuffle my feet and wipe my hands on my jeans, making sure all the cheese is off, and turn the doorknob to open the door.

A woman with chocolate hair and big brown eyes stares back at me. It takes me a second to recognize her, since I only saw her for maybe a minute, but my mouth drops open when I realize who it is.

Carmen's sister.

Ana.

My *aunt*.

"Mia?" she asks, a nervous look on her face.

I'm Mia. She said my name. Why am I not saying anything back?

I close my mouth and take a step back, my fingers hovering on the doorknob. I glance around for any sign of Carmen, but there is none. Why would my aunt be here? How does she know where I live? What the heck is going on? I need answers, but I don't know what to ask. So I say the first thing that comes to my mind instead.

"Um, hi?"

I don't know why that's my go-to phrase, but it is. And it's annoying. So, when she doesn't say anything, I try again. "What are you doing here?" I know I should have said something else, but my mouth speaks before my brain works sometimes.

"I wanted to speak with you. And your *familia*." Her beautiful Spanish accent is just as strong as my grandmother's was. The grandmother I met for two seconds. I wonder why Carmen doesn't have that thick of an accent. It's there, but barely.

"Why?"

"To apologize. For the way your mother . . . my sister

acted. And . . ." She holds up what looks to be a note or letter, adjusts her grip on the suitcase she has in her other hand, and gives me an expectant look. "May I come in? We need to talk."

CHAPTER 29

Happiness is always there, you just have to look for it.
Look inside your soul, you heart, your mind.
It's really not that hard to find.
—J.S.

"Mia? Who is it?" Dad's voice echoes through the house, but I'm too stunned to answer.

After the initial shock wears off, I manage to invite Ana in. She sets her suitcase down in front of her and looks up as Dad walks in the room.

I'm not sure what to expect. Yelling? Ignoring? Sighing? Instead, Dad surprises me. "Ana?" he says. "What are you doing here?"

"It's nice to see you, Russ."

"Have a seat," I say, gesturing to one of the couches in the front room. I glance at Dad, but he's watching Ana.

She sits on the couch and we sit across from her, both with questions on the tips of our tongues, but neither of us says anything.

"I'm sorry to show up so unexpectedly. I apologize I didn't call beforehand."

No words, just more staring.

She shifts, obviously uncomfortable with our eyes on her. "I . . . Mia, when you showed up at Carmen's home last week, I had so many questions I wasn't able to ask. Once I spoke with Carmen after you left, I got most of the answers I needed and the courage to act. I'm sorry I've been absent for nearly your entire life. There are no excuses. Only regrets."

Dad looks tired. "Ana, why are you really here?"

She plays with the letter still in her hand. "I'm here because I want to donate my kidney. I want to save my *sobrina's* life."

Dad glances at me and I try to talk, but I'm so shocked and so full of emotion that I just sit there. Dad puts his arm around my suddenly shaking shoulders.

"You came all this way for Maddy?"

She nods. "Of course. She's family."

Dad's eyes get teary and he clears his throat. "You—" He shakes his head. "You have no idea how much this means to us."

"All I want is to help the family I lost so many years ago. I know how much she hurt you. How much she took from you. And I'm so sorry."

Dad stands and crosses the room to wrap her in a hug. "Thank you, Ana. Thank you so much for coming and for caring about Madison so much." He pulls away.

"You're welcome."

I still can't speak. All I can do is wipe tears away and reach for a tissue.

"What do I need to do first?" Ana asks. "I'd like to get things done as quickly as possible."

"You'll have to get a blood test so they can match blood type and a bunch of other things before you're good to donate." Dad pulls out his phone. "Do you want me to call and schedule it?"

"Yes. That would be great."

"You can stay here if you'd like or we can put you up in a hotel downtown."

Ana smiles. "Thank you, but I have a room already. I may need a ride to get there, though. I just sent the taxi away."

"We can give you a ride, no problem." Dad walks away as he puts his phone up to his ear.

I'm still staring. "I don't really know what to say. When I left Carmen's house, I couldn't understand how she didn't care."

Ana clasps her hands in front of her. "I know."

"Thank you," I say.

"Don't thank me yet. We need to find out if I'm a match first."

I sniff and nod as she holds up the letter in her hand. "You need to read this."

"Okay?" I stand and take it from her.

Please don't be from Carmen. I can't handle anything she has to say.

Like she can read my mind, Ana says, "It's okay, Mia. It's not from her."

"Oh." My stress level just dropped five notches. "Thanks." The envelope is already open. Curious, I pull the letter out and I feel my eyes bug out as I read the contents.

240

Ms. Santalina,

You don't know me, but I was with your daughter, Mia, the night she came to visit you. I don't want to pry or get into business that's not mine, but I do want you to have this. Use it for a plane ticket and hotel. It should take care of that and then some. I can't do much for Mia and her sister, Maddy, but if money is the reason you can't fly to California, you don't have that excuse anymore. I hope you find it in your heart to do the right thing.

—J.S.

J.S. Jaxton Scott. I don't believe this. My eyes are blurry and I fight to keep the tears back. After swallowing the lump in my throat, I try to hide my emotion.

"How . . ." I start. "How much did he give you?"

"Enough." She folds her arms. "At first I didn't want to take it. But there was no return address, no name, nothing. So I thought about it. And thought about it. But there was no other way to get here, so I had to use it. I don't know who this friend of yours is, but whoever it is really cares for you."

Jax cares about me. He *really* cares. I don't know what to say. Or do. I could text him, but . . . I erased his number from my phone. I'm such an idiot.

"Did Carmen read this?"

She nods. "I found it in the garbage. The money was on the table, just sitting there. I asked her about it and she told me to take it. So I did." She pauses. "I've always known about you and Maddy, Mia. I had no idea you were so grown up. And when you came to see Carmen, I listened from the kitchen. I'm so sorry. I know I shouldn't have, but you're my family! When I heard your baby sister needed a kidney, I was horrified and so embarrassed that Carmen refused. Maddy is her daughter. I'm ashamed and so sorry she didn't help you. She's changed, my sister. I love her, but she's been through too much to come back."

She shakes her head as though shaking off a bad memory. "So . . . After you left and especially after I read that note, I tried to talk her into it. She wouldn't hear me out. So I made a decision. I booked a flight here and tracked down your family. I remembered the general area where you guys lived, but didn't know for sure, so I looked you up in the phonebook at the airport."

"Thank you."

"I don't know if I'll be a match, but if I am I'd be honored to donate a kidney to save Madison's life. It's the least I can do to make up for the silence Carmen has granted you with all these years."

If I was crying before, now I'm sobbing. Tears stream down my cheeks. "You don't have to do it just because of her."

"I'm not. You are family. Family is everything. And it's the least I can do. What's one less kidney anyway?" She smiles and takes my hand as I sit down next to her.

"Thank you."

"No," she says. "Thank *you*. You're an amazing young woman to do something so selfless for your sister. Going to New York and trying to find your mother when you never even knew her. It makes me proud to be your aunt." She smiles and wipes the tears trailing down her cheeks. "I just wish we could have gotten to know each other much earlier than this. Forgive me. I didn't have the courage to find you."

"It's not your fault."

"Partly. Carmen shut that part of her life out, and it in turn shut us out, as well. But I'm here now. And things are going to work out."

I don't have anything to add to that, so I just sit there, my hand in hers, my other one holding Jax's letter. I'm so overwhelmed with the amazing people in my life that I'm not sure to do with all this emotion.

Ana, for being so brave. Brave to give a piece of herself to another person.

Jax, for everything he did for me and everything he's continued to do. I try to ignore the feeling of my heart breaking in two as I think of him. Under all the happiness and emotion I'm feeling right now, the sadness takes over.

I miss him. I should text him. Thank him. Something.

But I realize then that I don't want to text him. I want to thank him in person. A text message seems so impersonal. No, doesn't seem so—it *is* impersonal. When this is all over, I'll find a way to see him again. To really, truly say thank you to his face.

CHAPTER 30

Don't lose hope, I'm on your side.
I'll sail with you across the tide.
The waves are rough, the storm is too,
We can weather it together. Just me and you.
—J.S.

The next week flies by. The whole family is at the hospital with Maddy when the doctor brings us the news.

I sit next to the bed, holding her hand. I swear my heart is going to beat out of my chest as he shuts the door and comes to stand at her feet.

He looks so calm. So . . . not happy. Which makes my stomach drop. But then he breaks into an easy smile and reaches out to shake Ana's hand. "You're a match."

I jump out of my chair and pump my fist in the air. I should probably be a little quieter or cry or something, but this is not time for crying. It's a time for celebrating. My sister is getting a new kidney. She's going to be okay.

"Mia. Relax," Dad says with a laugh.

"I'm just so excited!" I jump into Dad's outstretched arms and give him the biggest hug I can muster. I hug Mom next, and then my brother Zack. The last hug I save for Ana. She's the one person I never thought I'd be hugging. And when she wraps her arms around me, it's like a part of Carmen is in her. The (perhaps fictional) part of her that actually cares about me. And right now, that's enough.

Maddy lies in the hospital bed like she has for so many weeks. She's awake, but exhausted, so all I get from her is a tiny smile.

I'll take it.

"You're going to be okay," I say, taking her hands.

Tears fill her eyes, but she doesn't do anything but nod.

The doctor talks to my parents for a second before turning to the rest of us. "We're going to schedule the surgery in two days. Now that we have everything we need, we want to get things going before Maddy has any more complications." He looks at Ana. "Is that okay?"

She nods. "Yes."

"The recovery from the donor is usually worse than the recipient. Do you have people who can stay with you and help you recover for a while?"

I put my arm around her. "We'll be here with her the whole time."

He smiles and nods. "Perfect. I'll get this scheduled and we'll go from there. Congratulations, Maddy. You have an amazing family here."

She lifts her fragile hands and wipes tears from her eyes. "I know."

I still can't believe this is happening. Maddy's gonna be okay.

She's going to live.

CHAPTER 31

Fate. So much depends on that one little word.
—J.S.

The waiting room is nearly empty aside from Mom, Dad, and me. I scribble in my notebook, making lists of who knows what. Things to do after Maddy gets better, thank-you notes to write, friends to catch up with. I guess I could write *him*, but it would get lost in his millions of pounds of fan mail.

"How long has it been?" I ask for the fifteenth time.

Dad glances up from his phone. "Honey. It's been about two hours. Just like the last time you asked."

"Oh." I go back to my list-making. Or try to.

Maddy was nervous this morning. I don't know why she was so worried. The doctor said the surgery would be fine. But how can you totally believe something like that when you've been so sick for so long?

I stand and start pacing the room.

"Mia, why don't you go get something to eat?" Dad says.

"No way. I want to be here when she's done."

Mom stands and puts a hand on my arm. "Honey, go relax for a little bit. Only one person can go see her when she's done anyway. You have some time to kill."

My stomach rumbles and I frown. I didn't realize how hungry I am until now. I know I didn't eat breakfast, but I don't eat breakfast a lot, so it's usually not a big deal. I cringe as it growls again and then I relent. "Okay. Maybe I'll just go see what they have." I walk to the elevators, press the button, and step inside when the doors open.

Where am I going again? Oh. Right. Breakfast. I don't really feel like eating, though. I feel kind of . . . nauseous. Anxious? Mom and Dad wanted me to go do something, though, so I have to do *something*. Where the heck do they want me to go? I don't have anything to do. Nowhere else to be. This is stupid.

Once I reach the front lobby, the doors open. Three people wait for me to get off, but I just stand there and stare at them. They step inside and, instead of getting out, I push floor number 2 and go back up. I step out of the elevator, walk back in the waiting room, and sit down on the couch across from Dad. He doesn't even glance at me. All he says is, "Told you she'd be back."

Mom chuckles. "Do I really owe you five bucks?"

He puts his paper down with a grin. "It was a bet, wasn't it?"

I glare at both of them. "Really? You bet on me? You guys must be super bored."

"We are," they both say at the same time.

Dad rubs his fingers together. "Pay up, ma'am."

She lets out a huff before she gets out of her chair and pulls out her wallet. Once she finds a five-dollar bill, she slaps it into his hand. She tries to walk away, but he pulls her into his lap and kisses her instead.

"Geez, guys. I'm sitting right here." I'm used to their PDA, but we're in a hospital for crying out loud.

Dad glances over Mom's shoulder. "You shouldn't have come back then."

I smile, pull out Jax's MP3 player, and turn on his music to tune them out. Yes, his music. I'm such a sucker for a handsome face. And his screaming is growing on me. Just a little. Blue Fire will never be in my top ten. I do enjoy the ballads, though. There are three of them on this particular CD, which I love, because they showcase Jax's real voice. Not the screamy weird one. I sink down into the couch and lean my head back, closing my eyes as Jax serenades me.

I wonder how he's doing. Has he figured out how to live his life the way he wants to? I miss him. Which still sounds so dumb. I only knew him for what? Three days?

With my earbuds in and music blasting in my ears, my eyes get droopy. And before I know it, the world goes dark.

♫

Someone's shaking me.

"What the—" I sit up and rip the earbuds out. "Mom?"

"She's done."

I wipe a little drool off my cheek, hoping she didn't notice. "What? How long has it been?"

She smiles. "You've been asleep for two hours."

Two hours? "Whatever." I don't take naps. Ever. And now I realize why I don't. I feel like someone knocked me out. My head is pounding and my stomach feels like it's trying to scratch its way out of me.

I'm starving.

"I'm serious. The doctor just came to talk to us. Dad went to the recovery room with Maddy. They'll let us go back in a little bit."

How the heck did I sleep that long? And why did no one wake me up? "Okay." I'm kind of disoriented still, so I blink a few times, ignore the dude sitting a few chairs over who's staring at me like I'm some kind of freak for sleeping in the hospital waiting room, and stretch. My muscles are tight, especially my neck. Stupid couch.

A nurse walks into the room and heads straight for Mom. "Everything went great. She's awake if you'd like to see her. Ana is still asleep, but I'll let you know as soon as she wakes, as well."

"Thanks," Mom says, and we follow the nurse back to Maddy's room.

She's surrounded by monitors, as always, and she's a little pale, but she's awake. And even better, she's smiling. "Hey," she says as she looks up.

"You okay, sweetie?" Mom kisses the top of her head and fusses over her for a few minutes. I stand back with my arms folded and watch them. Warm fuzzies making me smile.

"Hey, Mia." Maddy reaches out for me and I scoot past Mom to take her hand. "I'm done."

"I know. How are you feeling?"

"I'm a little loopy from the meds, but I think I'm okey-dokey."

"Okey-dokey?"

She giggles. "Like I said. The meds." She lets out a slow breath and moves around to get herself comfortable.

"You okay?"

"Sore. And loopy. I think it's the meds," she repeats as a big, goofy grin makes its way across her face. But then she frowns like she's in pain.

"Do you need anything?"

She shakes her head. "No. I don't think so. Just sleep."

"Okay. I'll let you sleep."

She smiles and pulls her hand away. "Did your boy-friend call you?"

My cheeks heat as Dad shoots me a look across the room. I try to keep my face neutral. "What?"

"You know. The rocker you spent the night with or whatever."

"Mia?" Dad asked, his voice panicked and concerned at the same time.

"What are you talking about?" How does she know about Jax? I shake my head at her, hoping she'll keep it to herself, but all she does is gives me that goofy grin again.

"He's hot. I'm kind of jealous. Actually not kind of. Super jealous."

"Maddy . . ." I say, trying to make her stop.

She laughs and then makes a pained expression. "Okay. No laughing. That hurts." She closes her eyes. "So tired."

"Go to sleep."

"Okay. Talk later."

She's out in seconds.

I feel Dad's eyes on me and I attempt to sneak out of the room, but he catches my arm before I make it to the door. "What's this about a rocker boyfriend?"

I sigh. "Dad, I don't have a boyfriend."

"Then what was she talking about?"

"No idea. Must have been the meds."

CHAPTER 32

The days go by as I lay in bed
Songs of loneliness run through my head
The demons thought they defeated me
I've let them go. I've been set free.
—J.S.

Hours later, I'm sitting in Maddy's room reading a book, waiting for her to wake up. I glance over at her and see her eyes closed again, so I reread the same paragraph I've already read ten times. I can't concentrate. I have to know if she's going to be okay.

I set the book down as she moves, and a few seconds later, opens her eyes. She glances around and smiles when she sees me. "Hey." Her voice is scratchy, but it's the best sound in the world.

"Hey."

"How long have I been out?"

"A couple hours."

"Feels like days." She moves and winces. "Losing and gaining an organ is kind of painful."

I chuckle. "I'll bet it is."

"I didn't say anything stupid earlier, did I? I remember waking up, but I don't remember what I said."

I, on the other hand, know exactly what she said. "Um, you said stuff about me. And a certain . . . rocker?"

A grin spreads on her face. "Right. I remember that now."

"That was weird, right?"

She chuckles a bit, but grimaces from pain. "Not weird. The truth."

My eyes grow wide. "Who told you? I swear I didn't tell anyone."

"No one told me silly." She looks around the room. "Could you hand me that for a sec?" She points to her laptop on the table across her room. I grab it and set it on her lap, wondering what I'll find when she opens it. "Why didn't you say anything about it when you got back?"

"About what?"

"Oh, don't play dumb, Ms. Jaxton Scott. I know everything."

"Okay. Now you're freaking me out."

"Why didn't you tell me?"

"I didn't want anyone to know. Are you going to tell me how you found out?" I lean closer but can't see the screen.

She types in a few words, waits for a moment, and turns the laptop to face me. "You know how much I love Hollywood news. Imagine my surprise when I was scrolling through recent stories and I saw this."

I can't help myself—I actually gasp. There on the screen is a picture of Jax and me sleeping on the plane on the way to New York. "How did . . .?"

"Oh, just you wait. There's more." She smiles as she scrolls down to reveal a picture of Jax and me walking through Central Park. Then one of us standing near the guitar player, which, if I'm being honest, is super cute. And there's another one of us holding hands as we race away from the paparazzi. My hair, thankfully, is covering my face in that one. Another one at the pizza place, where Jax and I stand near the piano I played. My hands are over my mouth, but you can tell I'm smiling, and Jax is in the middle of clapping his hands with a huge grin on his face and his eyes only on me. After staring at that one for a while, I look at another taken of us at Ground Zero.

"Seriously? Who took these?"

Maddy laughs, but winces again and settles down. "I don't know, but I'd like to thank whoever did."

I glare at her and then turn my attention back to the pictures. This time, I read the captions and groan.

Who is this mystery girl?
Sorry ladies, Jaxton Scott has a new woman.
Jaxton Scott spotted with mystery girl at Central Park.
Looks like the lead singer of Blue Fire is out and about with a new woman.

Ice cold dread rushes through me as I scroll through every picture. "Do Mom and Dad know?"

"Not yet. They don't pay attention to stuff like that."

I sigh in relief. "Good. Dad's going to kill me if he finds out. He almost killed me when you blurted out that I had a rocker boyfriend earlier."

"I said that?"

"Yes. I blamed it on you being doped up on medication."

"Nice save."

"Barely."

Maddy smiles. I can tell she's still tired, but she's more herself than she's been in forever. "I can't believe it. My sister was with Jaxton Scott. You were holding hands with Jaxton Scott."

I blush. "Crazy, right?"

"Care to enlighten me with a few stories? You know he's my favorite in Blue Fire."

"Not really."

"Oh, you're gonna tell me everything." She moves the bed up just a tad, but cringes and stops. I move it back down, help her adjust her pillows behind her, and set an extra one next to her to rest her arm on. Anything to keep her comfortable. "This is freaking Jaxton Scott. Lead singer and guitarist of Blue Fire. How the heck did you, out of all the women in New York, end up hanging out with him?"

I put my face in my hands, feeling my cheeks heat. "We sat next to each other on the plane there." I look up at her, a grin on my face. "And you won't believe what I said to him."

"Tell me everything."

And I do.

CHAPTER 33

Take control of your life. It's yours. Just yours.
No one else can do it for you.
When things get tough, don't give in, don't give up.
Save yourself before it's too late.
Find a reason to live. Be strong, be brave.
You're the only one who can change your fate.
—J.S.

It's been three days since her surgery, and Maddy's doing amazing. She's up and walking around, slowly, while I drag her IV stand everywhere she goes, but at least she's up. She gets tired easily, though, of course, but she's not exhausted like before. And she has more color. She says she's really sore, but feels good.

Ana's doing well, too, although she's having a harder time with the pain.

Today we sit in Ana's room, me in one chair, Maddy in the other, and tell stories of our childhood to pass the time. Hopefully Ana can get better fast and she can go home to New York. I can tell she misses it. Her sister, too.

"Remember that one time when you got in the wrong car at the grocery store?" Maddy says.

"No . . . ?" I lie. Of course I remember. I even shut the door and tried to put the key in the ignition. It was a good thing no one saw me. "Remember when you walked in on Mr. Forester and Miss Hodges making out in the teacher's lounge in junior high?"

She laughs. "Yeah. *That* was awesome. They both gave me A's the rest of the year."

"To keep you quiet."

"Like I would have told anyone. I was scarred for life that day. I don't care if they're single and have the hots for each other. Seeing your teachers like that? Gross."

I chuckle at the disgusted look on her face. "You told me."

She snorts. "You're different."

"True. But still. I could have told the whole school."

"But you didn't. Because sisters keep sisters' secrets. It's in the sister pact."

I slap my hand against my forehead. "Oh, geez. The sister pact?"

Ana chuckles in her hospital bed. "You girls are hilarious. I could listen to you all day."

Maddy glances at the TV and reaches across me to grab the remote. "Ouch."

"Seriously? Let me do it!" I hand it to her.

She changes the channel. "I forget small movements like that kill me every time I move. I'm so used to just reaching for things. It's annoying." She smiles. "I know it will heal, though. Oh, look! Right on time. My favorite show is on."

"Ugh, really? You're going to watch this here?" I groan again as the Hollywood entertainment show comes on.

"You know how much I love the news."

"This is not news. This is stupid gossip."

"This is not gossip. They give lots of facts about celebrities. It's interesting." She grins. "And you should pay attention to it anyway, Ms. Scott."

"Right." Ms. Scott. Jax and I aren't even dating. "About that . . ."

"Yes, about that. I'd like to show you something I found while you were in New York."

Even so, I watch it with her. Just to make her happy, of course. And to maybe catch a glimpse of Jax if they feature him. As the show starts, though, I roll my eyes as the hosts go on and on about different celebrity breakups, hook-ups, pregnancies, fights, who's in rehab, who's having a nervous breakdown, etc. In other words, nothing important. Or interesting.

When I see Jax's friend Melanie on the screen, posing at some awards show, I can't handle it anymore. "Can we please turn it?" I beg, reaching for the remote.

"Wait," Maddy says. "Look."

I glance back at the TV, surprised to see Jax's picture in the top right corner. "Some breaking news this week about Jaxton Scott, the lead singer of Blue Fire. He announced on Tuesday that Blue Fire is breaking up. We all knew there was drama within the group, but didn't see it breaking up for good so soon. Jaxton, it seems, wants to focus on a solo career. The other members of Blue Fire had no comments when we spoke to their representatives. Best of luck to the band and their now heartbroken fans."

"He really did it," I whisper. My fingers dig into my chair and I feel Maddy's eyes on me.

The reporter continues. "Right after his big announcements, Jaxton uploaded an original song on the Internet and it's already gone viral with over 1 million hits."

My eyes are glued to that TV as it shows a clip of him singing with his guitar. He looks amazing. Eye-brow ring and all.

The host of the show continues. "The song, title unknown, features him singing a solo while strumming his guitar. It's a beautiful song, but he hasn't commented on why it was written or for whom. If you want to check it out, here's the link to the website."

"Write that down," I yell to no one in particular and dive out of my chair. I can't find anything that resembles a piece of paper or a pen. "Seriously? No pen?" I check my purse.

Both Ana and Maddy ignore me, eyes glued to the TV.

"No word, either, on what's going on with Blue Fire or the mystery girl he was seen with a few weeks ago." A picture of Jax and me at Central Park flashes on the screen and my mouth drops open. "Any attempts to reach Mr. Scott or Blue Fire have not been answered."

My freaking face was just on TV.

The story ends and Maddy mutes it. No one speaks for at least a minute.

"So. *That* was interesting. I take it you know that boy, Mia?" Ana asks.

I look over at her and give her a half smile compared to the huge smile she's giving me. "Sort of?" Thank goodness my parents aren't in here.

"You didn't tell me the writer of that letter was famous."

"I didn't think it was important."

She chuckles. "Well, are you going to look up the song or not?"

"I couldn't find a pen so I didn't write it down."

"I have it on my phone," Maddy says, handing it to me. "Just push play."

I stare at the phone. Why am I freaking out right now? And why didn't I think to use my phone? Seriously. Who doesn't just look it up on their phone? I must be losing my mind.

"Well?" they both say.

My finger hovers over PLAY and finally, after what seems like forever, I push the button.

Jax's face appears on the screen. He's not wearing a hat, so his dark hair is messy and adorable. He holds his guitar and stares straight at me. Or . . . The screen. Yeah.

"Hey, everyone. I wanted to share this song with you today. It means a lot to me. It's about a very special some-one, who I hope will hear it and understand what I'm trying to say."

He lets that hang in the air for a moment and then looks down at his guitar. "Here we go."

Music flows from his guitar. Beautiful, amazing, per-fect. A melody that reaches into my soul and tries to carry me away. And just when I think it can't get any better, he opens his mouth to sing.

Words not meant to remain unsaid.
Fight their way through my clouded head.
You're the one who set me free.
Vanquished the demons haunting me.
You changed me more than words can say.

A debt which will take all my life to repay.
Fly away with me, your soul set free.
Whatever you dream of, together we'll be.
Let's walk among the stars tonight.
Leave darkness behind, step into the light.

Your smile, your touch, your everything.
Peace to my soul is what you bring.
I hear your voice, begging me to stay.
To leave my old life and run away.
There's no place on earth I'd rather be.
Than right here and now, just you and me.

Fly away with me, your soul set free.
Whatever you dream of, together we'll be.
Let's walk among the stars tonight.
Leave darkness behind, step into the light.

He strums the last few notes and the video fades to black. I have no words. I hear sniffing behind me and look to see Ana and Maddy both wiping tears away.

"That was so beautiful," Maddy says.

I stare at her. It couldn't be for me, could it? Why

would he write it right after we met? Or did he write it for someone else before he met me and then uploaded it to get everyone's attention off the band's breakup story? What is going on?

"You need to call him."

"I can't! I deleted his number."

"What?" they both yell.

"I didn't think I'd ever see him again. And besides, didn't you hear the story? I have no idea where he is or what he's doing. He told me at the airport he needed time." I frown.

"Time for what?"

"To figure out his life. What he wants."

Maddy rolls her eyes. "It's obvious he wants you."

"Right."

She gives Ana a look that I choose to ignore.

"Do you think he wrote that song because he was too afraid to tell you how he felt in person?" Ana asks.

Jax? Scared? Ha. He sings in front of millions of people and doesn't even break a sweat. No. I don't believe that for a second. "Why would he be scared? I'm not scary."

"You are. A little," Maddy says.

I put my face in my hands. "I don't know what to do."

Maddy pats me on the back. "It's going to be okay. We'll figure it out. If he went through all that trouble writing a song for you, he'll figure out a way to see you again."

"Right." I'm still not convinced that song is for me, but whatever. At least he's figuring things out with his life. He's doing something for himself and not for someone else.

"I'm hungry. Anyone want some Italian ice?" Maddy grabs a menu off Ana's table.

"Strawberry sounds *fabuloso*," Ana says.

"Yes," Maddy agrees. "Yes, it does. Although I do like the pina colada. It's a toss up."

While they talk about Italian ice flavors and which ones are the best, I listen to Jax's song again. What if he did write it for me? How do I feel about that?

So amazing there are no words to describe it.

I need to find a way to see him again.

CHAPTER 34

Stop your worrying and face your fears.
Laugh. Cry. Live. Love.
Stay true to yourself though it may be hard.
Always carry on.
You only have one life to live.
Be sure you live it well.
Take a chance, be brave, be strong.
It will be worth it in the end.
—J.S.

The airport is crowded as we stand in the main terminal. Ana looks great, though she still has a little pain, even
after six weeks. I'm sure she will for a while, seeing how
she just had an organ removed from her body.

That sounded super morbid.

"Are you sure you're okay? I wish we could walk you
to your gate." She picks up her carry-on and slings it over
one shoulder.

"I'm fine, Mia. *Promesa.*"

I smile. "That means promise." She's taught me a tiny
bit of Spanish since she's been here, although I only know
like three words. I need to get on that. It's part of me. A

part of my heritage. And now, I don't want to let it go. I'm going to miss her being around. I'm glad she decided to stay so long.

"*Si*." She glances at her watch and then nods at me. "Keep practicing, and the next time I call, I'll speak only in Spanish."

"Uh . . ."

She laughs. "Don't worry. I'm just joking." She takes a moment and searches my face. "I don't want to do this, but it's time to say good-bye." She hugs me tight. "Thank you for everything you've done. For all you'll do. I'm so proud of you. And I know, deep down, my sister is proud of you, too. She may not see it now, but I guarantee she'll see it later. There's no way she can't." She pulls away but still hangs onto my arms. "You're such an amazing woman. Life has good things in store for you. I know it."

"Thank you, Ana. For everything." I turn away as she says good-bye to Maddy. They're both crying. Of course they are. They share a bond more powerful than anything I can imagine. Ana saved Maddy, and I guess I, in a way, saved Ana. The guilt she felt for never getting to know us is still there, but it's softened now. And I'm so happy it has. She's a feisty, strong woman. And after nearly six weeks of getting to know her, I'm really going to miss her.

We watch as she says good-bye to our parents and then goes up the escalator. She gives us one last wave before she disappears.

"Well, that was sad," I say, draping my arm around Maddy's shoulders.

She's still wiping tears away. "I can't believe she did that for me. I really can't. I never even knew her at all and she saved my life? What can I do to repay something like that?"

I smile. "You can write her. Email. Keep in touch. That's all she needs, I think."

She nods, her eyes still misty.

Dad puts his arm around the both of us and kisses our heads. "I'm so happy my girls are back together, happy, healthy. I could just burst out into song or something."

"Dad," I say with a groan. "Please. Not here."

"Why not? I could get that guy over there to play his guitar for me and I'll sing." He points straight ahead and I laugh as my eyes fall on a guy with a guitar standing near the glass doors. He's wearing a baseball cap and has a tattoo around his bicep.

Jax.

I can't believe what I'm seeing. He's here? In California? How did he get here? I shake my head. A plane. Duh. The question is *why* is he here? I don't realize I've stopped walking until Dad gives me a little shove. "It's okay, Mia. I don't think he bites."

Maddy giggles behind me, but I don't turn around. All I can do is stare at Jax, who's looking at me like I'm the only person in the entire world.

Dad rests his hand on my back. "We'll meet you in the car. Don't take too long." And with that, he and the rest of my family leave me standing in the middle of the terminal, my eyes locked on a boy I thought I'd never see in person again.

Jax takes a few steps toward me, and I can't seem to make my feet move. I'm stuck. Trapped in a place of wonder and confusion. Emotions seem to come from everywhere, slamming into me, almost knocking me over. I don't move. All I can do is put my hand over my mouth to try to stop the sob that escapes, but of course it doesn't help.

I finally get my feet to move and instead of walking like the normal, sophisticated person I should be, I run to him and throw myself into his arms.

He buries his face in my hair as he sets his guitar case down, still hanging on to me with one arm. "Don't cry," he whispers.

"I'm not," I gasp as tears flow freely now. So embarrassing. I annoy myself with my emotional ways. I pull away from him and get a good look at his face as he sets me on the ground. "How? Why?" My brain isn't working. I don't know what to say. I don't know what to feel. I don't know how to describe the emotions taking over, the happiness, the joy, the fear. It's all there, laid bare for everyone to see. But for a small moment, I don't care. All I care about is him right now. He's here. With me.

"I've been planning this moment for a while now. After your sister called me a few weeks ago, we figured out the place and time. And from the looks of things, I take it the surprise worked pretty well."

I look around, wondering if my family really did go to the car or if they're watching us from somewhere close by. I don't see them. "Maddy called you? How? Why? How did she even get your number?"

"Silly girl. Phone records."

Duh.

He shrugs. "I was planning on seeing you again anyway. While I was figuring things out with my career, I couldn't stop thinking about you. And trying to figure out how to find you. I had your name and number, so I guess I could have called, but I wanted to see you again in person."

"What if I have a boyfriend now? It's been almost two months, after all." His face falls for a second and I can't keep my smile in.

"Then I would have tried to steal you from him."

I let that sink in, not knowing what to say to that. "So, you broke up your band."

He smiles. Sad and happy. If that's possible. "I did."

"How does it feel? The freedom?"

"Well, after a million hits on my first unofficial solo single, I think I'll be okay."

"How did you get out of your contracts."

"I have a good agent who looked between the lines. We compromised with our record label, did a bit of negotiating, and I fired my manager, who has run us into the ground ever since we started touring. Things just happened to work out when I set things in motion. It was scary, and I'm a little sad about my band not playing together anymore, but I feel so much peace about the whole thing. I haven't felt so right about something for a long time."

"I'm so happy for you."

"I'm excited and nervous for the journey ahead. It may be hard, but if I'm happy and doing what I love, that's what matters."

"I'm proud of you."

"Thanks." He touches my chin, sending chills down my body. "I knew I'd never be happy with the way I was living. Even before I met you. You just helped me speed up the process a little. You kicked my butt to actually do something about it. Thanks for that."

"You're welcome." I back away and fold my arms, still reeling about the fact that my whole family knew about this and I didn't have a clue. I don't like surprises. They know that. "You know, you could have texted me or something. You didn't have to come all the way here. I would have texted you back."

He snorts. "Texting isn't personal. Seeing someone, touching them, talking to them." He tucks my hair behind my ear. "Looking in someone's eyes. That's personal. Texting is just a way to say important things in a convenient—or I think the word I'm looking for is *lazy*—way. Or easy way. Getting on a plane to tell a person how you feel about them, that's much more effective than a text message."

I grasp onto his last words and my heart speeds up. I feel the same way. About all of it. "And how do you feel about me?"

He looks at me like *duh*. "I told you I don't date a lot, and I was serious. I don't get attached. But after spending time with you, and especially when you left, you kind of took my heart with you. Cheesy, yes, but sometimes the truth sounds cheesy."

It's anything but cheesy right now. But I don't tell him that. "That song. Was it . . ."

He grins. "It was for you."

Words can't begin to express how much I love the song, so I stare at him, still not believing.

Noticing how tongue-tied I am, he continues. "After you got on the plane, I didn't really know what to do with myself. You gave me so much to think about. You helped me see what I really wanted out of my life. I wanted a fresh start. I didn't want to sing with Blue Fire anymore. I didn't want to tour and stay on the road for months at a time. I didn't want to live the Hollywood lifestyle anymore." He smiles. "I'm done with it. What I want . . ." He trails off and his voice softens. "What I want is to make my own way in this world. Write my own music. Even if it doesn't go platinum or whatever. I just want to do what I want. And I want to be with you. Just you. To take you on a real date. To stay up for hours just to talk to you. To get to know you. I told you at the airport in New York that I believe in fate. And the second I met you on that plane, I knew fate had given me a break. Something to work for. To hold onto. So here I am. Clean and ready to move on with my life. It won't be as glamorous as before, but I hope you're okay with that."

"Uh, yeah I'm okay with that."

He laughs as he looks at my expression. And, honestly, I'm not sure what I look like. Confused? Awestruck? In love maybe? Maybe?

"Why me?" Is all I can manage to get out.

"Because you're real."

"But—"

"All I've ever wanted is to have is something real. And you are that something."

"But your music—your life! I'm a nobody. I'm not one of those glamour girls. Gorgeous girls. I'm just Mia."

He grabs my hand and pulls it to his lips. "I know."

Which brings me back to thinking about what he did for Maddy. "Jax, what you did for my family. I can't . . ." My lip quivers and tears threaten to spill over again.

"I didn't do anything any other decent person wouldn't do."

No one else would have done that. No one else would have given someone he didn't even know a handful of money for plane tickets and a hotel. He can have his pick of anyone—*anyone*—and he's chosen me. There's no way this is real.

Jax leans closer, trying to figure out what I'm thinking maybe. "You can tell me to go home if you want. Just say the words and I'll do it."

I shake my head. "I don't want that." At all.

"That's good. But I want you to know right now that I'm not perfect. Never have been. I'm a work in progress. We all are, I think. But if you'll give me a chance, I'll be the person you want me to be."

I stare at him. He's asking me if I'll give *him* a chance? Is he joking? Because there's no way I'd turn this boy down. Ever. I take his hand to pull him closer, wrap my arms around him and breathe in his scent. "I want you to be you, Jax. That's all. Just Jax."

"Hopefully you won't get sick of me then." He hugs me back and I can't even handle all the feelings right now. I just know that he's here. And he's real.

I pull away, but we're closer now than before. "So, what now? What are you going to do?"

He shrugs. "I have a few more shows to play with Blue Fire to finish our tour for good and then we're going our separate ways. Which is the direction it was going the whole time, so it's not a huge surprise for our fans. As for me, I want to go to college. Preferably, if you're okay with it, close to wherever you go."

"I still have a year of high school left."

"So?"

"I *was* thinking of maybe graduating early."

"You'll be in college with me before you know it."

A smile creeps to my lips. "What would you major in?"

"I don't know. I was thinking of being a nerd and majoring in music. But you already knew that."

I slap his arm. "I'm not a nerd."

He pulls me close. "We can be nerds together." I feel his breath tickle my ear. "You know . . . I've been thinking about that kiss back at the airport in New York. In fact—" He pulls away, just enough that we're basically nose to nose. "I can't get it out of my head."

I've thought about it every day since. But I'm not about to tell him that. My cheeks flush anyway with the memory buzzing through my head. "Sorry about that. I'm not usually so bold."

"Don't apologize. It was . . . Amazing." He leans closer, his lips an inch or two away, and as soon as they touch mine, it's like fire and ice and magic and sprinkles all rolled into one. Which is completely insane, but as I melt into him, smelling him, tasting him, it makes perfect sense to me. And that's all that matters.

It's like in those movies when a couple reunites at the airport and they confess their love for each other and kiss like no one's watching. Making all of us chick-flick lovers sigh breathily.

But for real. It's like that. And I love it. So much. His arms, already wrapped around my waist, tighten, and I feel myself smile as someone whistles at us.

He smiles too as we break apart, glances around at the audience we've acquired, and takes my hand in his. "Let's get out of here." He ignores the people taking pictures of him and kisses me again before we walk through the crowd and out the door to meet my family.

They're waiting next to the car, and Dad and Jax shake hands like they're best friends. Which is weird. I still have to talk to them both about going behind my back like that.

Maddy grins like the Blue Fire fan she is as he introduces himself to her, and Zack gives him a few high fives and starts talking about Legos or something, and Mom, Mom just smiles at us. Which is all I need from her right now. A smile can say so many things, especially when no words can adequately describe the way you feel.

"Not sure about that eyebrow ring," Dad says.

"Dad . . ." I start, embarrassed.

Jax doesn't look offended at all. "No worries. I was thinking of taking it out anyway."

"No!" I yell and blush at the look he gives me. "I like it."

Dad glances between us, sighs, and doesn't say another word about it.

After standing around in the airport parking lot forever, we finally get in Mom's SUV and head for home.

Mom and Dad in the front. Maddy and Zack in the middle and me and Jax in the back.

We talk and laugh and everything's wonderful. And as I sit there, I realize how precious and fragile life is. How small acts of kindness and love have made me strong enough to endure anything that comes my way.

Maddy's alive. She's going to be okay. And it all started with a tiny shred of hope that one person could save her. Hope. I had it all along, even when I thought it had disappeared. And even though the person I thought I could maybe count on didn't save Maddy's life, someone unexpected stepped up and took the challenge.

There are still good people in this world.

I think back to the last few weeks and smile. I have an aunt who loves me, even though my own mother never could. An aunt who was selfless and brave and gave Maddy the greatest gift anyone could ever give: a second chance at life. I have a family who loves me. Who loves Maddy. And then there's my wonderful boy. A boy who changed my life in just a few days simply by being himself. A boy I can't wait to spend time with and laugh with and talk with and go through struggles with.

Go to college with.

A boy who wrote a song just for me and cared enough about a girl he just met to help save her sister's life.

A boy who learned he was the only one who could save himself and turn his life and dreams around.

And he's mine.

My life is mine. And I'm going to enjoy every second of it with the people I love most.

Hope is a beautiful, uncomplicated thing. Something I've never given much thought about. But right now, in this very moment, I've never been more grateful for it in my entire life.